# HOME SCHOOL

## CHARLES WEBB

WHEELER
WINDSOR
PARAGON

This Large Print edition is published by Wheeler Publishing, Waterville, Maine, USA and by BBC Audiobooks Ltd, Bath, England.
Wheeler Publishing, a part of Gale, Cengage Learning.
Copyright © 2007 by Charles Webb.
The moral right of the author has been asserted.

The text of this Large Print edition is unabridged.
Other aspects of the book may vary from the original edition.
Set in 16 pt. Plantin.
Printed on permanent paper.

**LIBRARY OF CONGRESS CATALOGING-IN-PUBLICATION DATA**

Webb, Charles Richard, 1939–
    Home school / by Charles Webb.
      p. cm.
    ISBN-13: 978-1-59722-731-5 (hardcover : alk. paper)
    ISBN-10: 1-59722-731-5 (hardcover : alk. paper)
    1. Home schooling — Fiction. 2. Grandmothers — Fiction. 3.
Mothers-in-law — Fiction. 4. Suburban life — Fiction. 5.
Westchester County (N.Y.) — Fiction. 6. Large type books. 7.
Domestic fiction. I. Title.
PS3573.E195H66 2008b
813'.54—dc22                                        2008000632

BRITISH LIBRARY CATALOGUING-IN-PUBLICATION DATA AVAILABLE
Published in 2008 in the U.S. by arrangement with St. Martin's Press, LLC.
Published in 2008 in the U.K. by arrangement with The Random House Group Limited.
U.K. Hardcover: 978 1 405 68724 9 (Windsor Large Print)
U.K. Softcover: 978 1 405 68725 6 (Paragon Large Print)

Printed in the United States of America
1 2 3 4 5 6 7 12 11 10 09 08

*For
Jack Malvern
an unselfish person*

*'I have never let my schooling interfere with my education.'*

— Mark Twain

# ONE

Elaine had frequently seen the woman around the small town of Hastings, New York, where they both lived. She was often in the company of a man — presumably her husband - - whom Elaine recognized as one of the vice presidents who sat behind a polished desk at the local bank. But Elaine had never spoken to her, so one morning when the woman wheeled her shopping cart up beside Elaine in the supermarket, stopping abruptly, Elaine's first reaction was to jump slightly.

'Excuse me,' the woman said, 'but aren't you the people who took your children out of school?'

Elaine looked back without answering.

'You're teaching your boys at home.'

'That's right.'

It was quiet a moment, then the woman said, 'I assume you know what you're doing . . .'

'I think so.'

'I hope so,' she said, 'because our daughter was home from college and said if we'd done that to her she'd never have spoken to us again.'

A response came to Elaine's mind, which she suppressed, at least to begin with, and if the woman had said no more Elaine's statement would have remained unuttered. Unfortunately, however, she did say more.

'I asked Claire — what in the world could motivate parents to deprive their children of the happiest experience of their lives?' She looked at Elaine a moment longer, then pushed her cart past her and toward the bakery section.

'Excuse me,' Elaine said after her, 'did you want an answer?'

The woman stopped, turning to look back. 'Not necessarily.'

'We took them out so they wouldn't grow up to be bankers.'

If given a chance to retract any statement made during the course of her lifetime, without thinking twice Elaine Braddock would have chosen the one made that morning to Marion Montgomery in the supermarket. Flippancy and pettiness were the most offensive of qualities to Elaine, and to have lowered herself to respond in kind to the woman's insults became a source of great self-reproach. Reproach for a lapse in what Elaine felt, at root, to be her loving attitude toward all Mankind, even its most obnoxious representatives.

And then, over the course of the months that followed, she came to regret the comment on less philosophical grounds, as in the minds of their neighbors, and of the town collectively, the belief became current that Elaine and her husband had in fact removed their children from school to prevent them from entering the banking profession.

So widespread did this opinion become that Elaine's husband Benjamin considered taking out a full-page ad in the local newspaper at one point to explain their reasons for teaching their children at home. But in the end he recognized that prejudices in the community toward their unconventional approach to education were probably inevitable, and he let it go.

However, the testy supermarket exchange never quite left Elaine's mind and, one day, even though it was long afterwards, she followed an impulse to turn in to the local bank and walk up to the large desk with the plaque reading, Jack Montgomery, Senior Vice President, and as the man seated behind it was finishing a call she said, 'I owe your wife an apology.'

Returning the receiver to the phone, the man looked up at her.

'I'm Elaine Braddock.'

'Yes?' he said.

'I said something to your wife in the supermarket I need to apologize for.'

There was a pause, then the man said, 'That was a year ago.'

'I realize that. But I hope you'll tell her I'm sorry for the comment.'

A button on the man's phone began flashing but he pushed it in and it stopped. 'I can tell her that.'

'And I apologize to you too,' Elaine said.

He nodded. 'Yes,' he said. 'Well, thank you.'

'I won't take up any more of your time.' She turned and walked out of the bank.

As far as Elaine was concerned the matter would have ended there, except that two mornings later a phone call came from Marion, and the banker's wife announced, as her husband had, that she also appreciated Elaine's gesture in making amends for the remark of a year ago. And this led, after a slightly awkward silence, to Elaine suggesting they get together, which they did, an hour later, at the coffee shop in town, where seated across the table from Elaine, Marion went more fully into her objections to home schooling.

'We just don't think they're being prepared for the real world,' she said. 'I'm sorry if you got the impression we don't think you're well meaning.'

Elaine raised her cup to her lips. 'The real world,' she said.

'That's our only concern.'

'Interesting.' Elaine took a sip and returned the cup to her saucer.

'What is?'

'That concept of the "real world". That's a good discussion subject for us.'

'For who?'

'The four of us.'

'Oh,' Marion said. 'Well I wasn't bringing it up as a discussion subject. I just wanted to be sure you were aware that —'

'I know,' Elaine said, 'but we incorporate everything that comes along into their education, and I can see that concept making a really lively topic.'

Marion looked at her a few moments, then tore open a sugar packet. 'Listen. I don't suppose you happened to see those people on the news last night, that family up in Vermont who are doing what you are.'

'The Lewis family,' Elaine said.

'You know them?'

'We went up to visit them once. They're well known in the movement.'

Marion emptied the sugar into her coffee. 'Did you know they were in court?'

'They're never out of court.'

'They were up on the steps of their courthouse yesterday, cursing and swearing at everyone in sight. Not the best advertisements for your cause.'

'Garth and Goya are very outspoken,' Elaine said, and then she turned and looked through the window beside their table and at the sidewalk outside and for a long time she just sat very still, staring through the glass, till finally Marion leaned forward slightly from the other side of the table.

'Elaine?'

'Yes,' she said, still not turning back.

'You okay?'

She looked back at her.

'I feel like I've lost you,' Marion said. 'Everything all right?'

Elaine shook her head. 'Not really.'

'Oh?'

'Something's happened.' It was quiet for another few moments, then Elaine said, 'Actually, maybe you could shed some light on it.'

'What is it?'

'Okay, some of the parents around town have begun complaining about us.'

'They have?'

'Have you heard anything about this?'

'Nothing.'

Elaine picked up her cup again.

'What did they say?'

'Do you know Principal Claymore at the school?'

'Ralph Claymore, of course.'

'I guess a group of them contacted him to say their children were upset by our situation.' There was another pause. 'But you haven't heard anything about this around town?'

'Nothing at all.'

'Benjamin's going up to meet with the school board about it, and if it turns out to be serious he'll take his month off from the library now so we can deal with it.'

'I've heard nothing,' Marion said, 'but that doesn't mean anything.'

Elaine took a sip from her cup. 'Of course Benjamin thinks they're making it all up.'

'Who is?'

'The school board.'

'Making what up?'

'About the other parents. Inventing it to get the boys back in school.'

'Oh no, Elaine.'

17

'He thinks we've become an annoyance to them and they've just concocted the story.'

'The board would never do that,' the other woman said. 'Do you believe that?'

'I just don't know.' Elaine turned her wrist so she could see her watch.

'It's out of the question, Elaine. Do you have to be somewhere?'

'Oh no.'

'You were looking at your watch.'

'Benjamin's just starting his meeting.'

When Benjamin arrived, it turned out there were only two others present for his meeting at the Westchester County Unified School District building in White Plains. Frank Anello, Superintendent of Schools, and Ralph Claymore, the principal of Warren G. Harding Elementary School, which Matt and Jason Braddock had attended up until three years before. The men were waiting for Benjamin in Superintendent Anello's office and rose from their chairs as a secretary showed him in.

'Principal,' Benjamin said, shaking the hand of the man nearest him.

'Hello, Ben.'

'Superintendent.' He shook the other man's hand.

The superintendent nodded at the free

chair on the other side of his desk and the three of them sat.

For several seconds it was quiet in the room.

'Frank and I were just commenting on that terrible flood out in Iowa,' the principal said finally. 'Have you been watching pictures of that?'

'We see the news.'

'Devastation on that scale,' the principal said, shaking his head, 'just breaks your heart.'

Again it was quiet till Superintendent Anello cleared his throat softly and nodded at the principal, who pulled his chair an inch or two closer to Benjamin's and, looking with a slight frown down at the carpet, said, 'Ben, we've had some reaction in the community to the home-education experiment you and your wife are conducting.'

Benjamin nodded.

'I assume your wife —— Elaine, is it?'

'Elaine.'

'She and I discussed all this on the phone. I assume she reviewed that conversation with you.'

'What were the reactions?' Benjamin asked.

'Of the community?'

'If you could be specific.'

Principal Claymore pursed his lips, then after a moment unpursed them again. 'Well Ben, I'm afraid some of our parents are having a little trouble adjusting to it.'

'To what?'

'To the home-schooling experiment.'

'Well, why do they have to adjust to it?' Benjamin said after another pause.

'Excuse me?'

'We're the ones who have to adjust to it.'

The principal tipped his head slightly to the side as he looked back at him.

'Okay, well what seems to be their problem with it?'

'It's not so much a problem, Ben — and, by the way, don't take this as a criticism of the wonderful, responsible way you and your wife have gone about it, that's the farthest thing from anyone's mind — but they just don't know how to explain to their youngsters why one family in the community doesn't have to send —'

Benjamin raised his hand slightly. 'If I may suggest this,' he interrupted, 'what I think we should do is meet with the families having the problems so my wife and I can answer their questions.'

Again the principal glanced at the superintendent, seated behind his desk, before proceeding. 'I wish we could do it that way,

Ben. But unfortunately they've asked us to keep their names out of it.'

'And this is just coming up now?'

'I'm sorry?'

'We've had them at home for three years. And this is just now coming up?'

'It's been simmering,' the superintendent interjected. The other two waited to see if he would say more, but he didn't.

'Okay,' Benjamin said, 'what you should do is tell them Elaine and I would like to host a discussion group at our home — bring their children along of course. I'm sure they'll be happy to reveal their identity if they know it's going to be a positive and informative exchange of ideas.'

The door to the office opened and the secretary looked in. The superintendent gave a shake of his head and she disappeared.

'Why don't we plan to do that?' Benjamin said.

'A round table,' Principal Claymore said.

'Call it that. Sure.'

The principal shook his head. 'Boy, don't I wish things were that simple.'

'Why aren't they?'

'Well as I told you — they've requested anonymity.'

'Right. So tell them they can come if they

choose to.'

'Boy oh boy, don't I wish it was that simple.'

'It is.'

The superintendent rolled a few inches forward in his chair. 'Mr Braddock, your boys need to be back in class in ten days. That's the Monday morning following Spring Break.'

There was a long silence, the two men looking at Benjamin as he sat studying one of his knees. 'Okay,' he said finally, looking up at the superintendent. 'First of all, if I'm not mistaken, our agreement with the school board is that as long as we abide by the conditions that were established . . .'

'It's a discretionary agreement,' Frank Anello said.

'Discretionary.'

'Wasn't that clear?'

'It was.'

'And we're exercising our discretion.'

Benjamin nodded. 'Okay,' he said. 'All right.'

It was silent as the two school officials continued watching him.

'Okay,' Benjamin said again. 'All right. Because of these parents that complained you're exercising it. So may I just find out a little more about these parents?'

'Let me just add something here,' the principal said, 'to put Ben's mind at ease. You know, Ben, all that learning and new thinking you've invested in those boys of yours over the last three years — that love of education you and your wife have instilled in them — is now going to come back up to school with them as a source of inspiration and enrichment not only for our other boys and girls, but for every last member of our teaching staff as well.'

'Exactly how did they approach you?' Benjamin said to the superintendent. 'These parents.'

Principal Claymore patted Benjamin's knee. 'Ben.'

'I'm asking him,' Benjamin said, moving his knee away. 'May I ask him?'

The principal withdrew his hand as Benjamin looked back across the desk at Superintendent Anello.

'Did they all show up at your office in a group? How did they all happen to get together at this particular time? Did they have a spokesperson?'

After a few more moments, Mr Anello reached forward to straighten a sheet of paper on his blotter. 'Mr Braddock, I'll repeat what I said before. From the outset it's been crystal clear to you and your wife that your agreement with the District is entirely discretionary and we can terminate it at any time.'

'That wasn't my question.'

'But it's my answer.'

'But who are these parents?' Benjamin said, getting to his feet. 'Why can't they be in touch with us directly if they want so badly to understand what we're doing?'

Again the secretary opened the door and looked in. The superintendent nodded. 'We're finished here, Martha.'

The drive between the School District building and Benjamin's house usually took half an hour, but he made it in twenty minutes, running two stop signs and once proceeding into an intersection well after the light had turned yellow so that to avoid a collision he had to slam on the brakes, angry motorists driving around him and yelling out their windows till the light turned green again.

Matt had been looking through the living-room window as his father drove into the driveway, and opened the front door as Benjamin came up onto the front porch. 'So what was the big meeting all about?' he said as his father walked past him.

'Where are Mom and Jason?'

'Doing history.'

'Can you tell them to come downstairs please?' He went into the kitchen and to a cupboard beside the sink, glancing behind him as he brought down a jar of instant coffee. 'Will you do that?' he said to Matt, who was standing in the doorway and looking in at him.

'What happened over there? You seem a little stressed.'

'I'm very stressed, Matt.' He opened the silverware drawer for a spoon, then transferred a large spoonful of the instant coffee to a cup. 'And getting more so as you don't go get the others.'

'They're studying the French Revolution.'

Benjamin turned on the water at the sink, running it till it was hot, then holding his cup under the tap.

'Is there a crisis or something?' Matt said, watching him stir the water as the cup filled.

'Yes Matt, there is a crisis.'

'What is it?'

'When everybody's down here I will go into it.'

'Do they want us to go back to school or something?'

Benjamin took a swallow from his cup.

'Dad?'

He nodded. 'That's their plan.'

'When?'

'In ten days.'

'Why?' Matt said.

'Because they're lying hypocrites.'

He watched his father take another swallow. 'That's the official reason?'

'Yes.'

'I'll get the others,' Matt said, turning toward the stairs.

But after a moment Benjamin called after him. 'Wait a minute.'

He stopped.

'Don't interrupt them after all. Come back.'

Matt returned to the doorway.

'Okay look,' his father said, raising his hand, 'first we need to get ahold of ourselves.'

'Speak for yourself.' He watched Benjamin finish the coffee and then spoon more of the brown powder into his cup. 'Are you ahold of yourself yet?'

'Yes.'

'And what about the crisis?'

'It's over.'

'I thought it just started . . .'

Benjamin held the cup under the tap.

'Dad.'

'What?'

'I thought the crisis just started.'

'And it just ended.' Benjamin stirred his new cup of coffee. 'Matt, you know how I'm always talking about turning dead-ends into opportunities? Well you're about to see that principle put into practice. The family's about to enter a new chapter.' He rinsed off the spoon to return to its drawer.

'What new chapter?'

'Remember the Lewis family? Up in Vermont? Garth and Goya and their two kids? When we visited them three years ago they said we could move into their cabin up there if something like this ever happened. You do remember them?'

'Those crazy people.'

Benjamin glanced at his son as he took a dish towel down from a hook. 'Matt, what have I said about labeling people?'

'Crazy?'

'Any label.'

'What about lying hypocrites?'

His father carefully dried the sides of his cup. 'And you need to learn the difference between labeling people and accurately describing their qualities.'

When the four of them had visited Garth and Goya and their children in Vermont, they had been invited to move into a second cabin on the Lewis property if insurmountable problems ever arose for Benjamin and Elaine with their local school authorities. This suggestion hadn't been considered before, but when Jason and his mother came down from studying it was introduced, and the rest of the day was spent discussing the possibility — arguing about it, more precisely — with Jason taking a favorable view, on the basis that any new experience should be tried out for its own sake, and Matt opposing the move, at least till he found out what television channels they got in Vermont.

Elaine's objections, however, were the most vociferous, as she repeatedly pointed out the absurdity of imagining they could transplant themselves into a remote and primitive environment. And as she and Benjamin went to bed that night, this continued to be the subject of discussion, Elaine calling to him from the bathroom as she brushed her teeth.

'Just from the health point of view,' she said, 'there's this little wood stove to heat the whole place, so we'd have colds all the time. You can't keep a place like that clean, so we'd all be covered with sores from top to bottom. Crawling things would be everywhere. Benjamin, we're suburban people and we depend on this life. I know you

28

don't like to admit that.'

He was sitting up in the bed, waiting for her to finish getting ready to join him. Having heard, and answered, all her current arguments, a response seemed unnecessary.

'You're in total denial to think we could survive five minutes up there.'

'I thought you liked Garth and Goya.'

'Well, I like what they stand for.'

'Then accept their gracious invitation. We'll overcome the minor difficulties and with their help we'll meet the challenge of a new life.'

Toothbrush in her mouth, Elaine stepped out of the bathroom so she could see him. 'Why do you keep talking about this? You know it's out of the question.'

'Then come up with a better idea.'

It was quiet for a few moments.

'Benjamin, we have almost two weeks to decide what to do.'

'Ten days.'

'That's what I said.'

'I thought you said "almost two weeks".'

'Same thing.'

'Elaine, who's in denial about what's happening? Really.'

Again it was quiet as they looked at each other.

'Well?' he said finally.

'Well what?'

'Come up with a better idea than Vermont.'

'I have.'

'I must have missed it.'

'You have a month off from the library and we have time to think about this.' She reached up to wipe a drop of toothpaste from her lip. 'We'll come up with something.'

He nodded. 'But if we can't, we move to Vermont.'

She went back into the bathroom. 'We're not mountain people,' she said. 'Whatever romantic fantasy you may have.'

'Oh, now they're mountain people.'

'All right, most mountain people don't have master's degrees, but you know what I mean.'

Benjamin looked down at the bedspread, then shook his head. 'Can you imagine Garth Lewis trotting up to some sell-out meeting with his school board like that? Anyone tells those two to put their kids back in school, he's out on the porch loading up his shotgun and she's next to him reading out the state trespassing statute.'

Elaine came back into the bedroom, turning down the spread on her side of the bed. 'They go about things in their way,' she said

30

as she got in, 'and we go about them in ours. We're all in the same fight.'

'Our way being to grovel, beg and roll over.'

'We need sleep, Benjamin.'

He sat without speaking as she got comfortable on her side of the bed, then finally turned his head to look down at her. 'Is it the Aaron thing?'

'What?'

'The reason you don't want to move up there. How much of it's the Aaron thing?'

'None of it.'

Benjamin nodded. 'You're hung up on the Aaron thing.'

'That has nothing to do with it.'

'Elaine,' he said, 'instead of being prejudiced toward them about that —'

'Benjamin.'

'Instead of being prejudiced, why not view moving up there as an opportunity to increase your tolerance of your fellow man?'

'I am fully tolerant of the Aaron thing.'

'Oh?'

'I am,' she said, turning to look at him. 'I just don't want to be around it.'

'That's your definition of tolerance, I take it?'

'And I'm not comfortable with Matt and Jason being around it.'

31

the ordinary the next morning that the family found itself in the back yard to discuss the possibility of Jason constructing a guillotine behind the house.

'And if you're so worried about the neighbors,' he said, walking over to the large tree in the yard, 'I'll make it over here so nobody can see it with all the leaves around it.'

'They'll see it when the leaves come off in the fall,' Matt said.

'I'll take it down by then.'

'Anyway,' Matt said, pointing at the house next door. 'Mrs Walker can see it from her upstairs window.'

'Mrs Walker can't see.'

'I think you need to build it inside, Jason,' his mother said.

'I told you, Mom,' he said, walking back to her, 'I can't get the height inside. That's the whole point — the blade has to drop down at least eight or nine feet and gather speed to chop off a head.'

'Sorry,' she said, 'I didn't realize it was for practical use.'

'Here's my suggestion,' Benjamin said. 'Build a miniature. And see if you can get it accurate in every detail.' He held his hand a foot or two off the ground. 'About this high.'

'What's the point of that?'

34

'To see if you can get it accurate in every detail,' his father repeated.

'Anyway, we can't get that kind of lumber,' Elaine said.

'He can take my Batmobile apart and use that lumber,' Matt said.

Benjamin shook his head. 'No guillotine in the yard.'

'Just because of the neighbors, right?'

'Partially.'

'I thought we didn't care what other people thought of us.'

'If they think we're chopping people's heads off,' Benjamin said, 'we care. Look —'

There was the sound of the front doorbell.

'I'll get it.' Elaine went into the house.

Benjamin was about to finish his sentence but their elderly neighbor, holding a broom, appeared on the other side of the picket fence that divided the two yards.

'Good morning,' she said.

'How are you, Mrs Walker?' Benjamin said.

'Is it a holiday? I see the boys are home.'

'We don't go to school,' Jason said.

'Oh?'

'I told her that yesterday,' Matt said.

'So? I'm telling her today.'

'Were your boys expelled?'

35

'We're going inside now, Mrs Walker,' Benjamin said. 'It was nice talking to you.'

There was one person who had disapproved of Benjamin and Elaine's decision to take their children out of school who didn't live in the community, or even the state for that matter, but three thousand miles away, and this was Elaine's mother. However, the effect of her disapproval was negligible, not only due to the distance that separated them, but also because she was legally required to greatly restrict her contact with the four of them, a condition resulting from certain indiscretions on her part that occurred when the family was also living on the other side of the country in California.

Coincidentally, though, and for no apparent reason, at this particular moment, just as the seemingly irrational demand by the school board was causing so much stress for them, she chose to send a gift to her grandchildren, an act which clearly violated the restricted access agreement which had been in place for five years.

And the first effect of the unauthorized gift (providing ample evidence of the disruptive force this woman could be in their lives) was to cause Elaine to do the one thing she and Benjamin put above all else never to do, which was lie to their children.

'So who was at the door?' Matt said as they came in from the yard.

'The postman.'

'Why did he ring the bell?' Jason said.

'A mistake — he was looking for someone on Circle Drive.'

It was several minutes later, after Jason and Matt had gone upstairs, and Benjamin, inspired by his neighbor, was on his way out the front door with a broom to sweep the driveway, that Elaine told him.

'That was a package from Mother,' she said.

He stopped.

'When the postman came.'

He turned around, looking at her a moment before speaking. 'A package came from your mother?'

'I had to sign for it.'

'Are you serious?'

'I know. I couldn't believe it either.'

'Where is it?' Benjamin said, leaning the broom against the wall.

'The closet.'

He opened the door of the closet beside him.

'On the shelf.'

Benjamin reached up to lift down the package. It was wrapped in brown paper, addressed to Jason and Matt, with the picture of a bunny their grandmother had drawn with a marker beside the address.

'You signed for it?' Benjamin said. 'Jesus Christ, why did you do that?'

'Benjamin, I didn't look to see who it was from. She's never done this before.'

He reached for the knob of the front door. 'I'll take it down,' he said.

'Down where?'

'Town. I'll drop it in a trash basket down there so they won't see it.'

'Why do that?'

'Because it is not going to stay in this house.'

She took it from him to look at the crude drawing on the front. 'What if we need it for evidence?'

'What in the fuck is that woman up to now?'

'Testing. Seeing what she can get away with. You know how she is.'

'But why now?'

'Who knows?'

He took it back, held it up next to his head and shook it. 'Evidence. You're right.'

'What do you think's in it?'

'Clothing or something.'

'Should we open it?'

Benjamin bent down and pulled some

38

boots and an umbrella back from the rear wall of the closet, then set the package down in the far corner. He put the boots and umbrella on top of it, then removed a heavy coat from a hanger and rested it on top of the boots, umbrella and package. 'No.'

'And don't tell them.'

'Of course not.'

'What if we sent it back to her unopened?' Elaine said as he backed out of the closet.

'Don't give her the satisfaction of getting a rise out of us.' He closed the closet door and pointed at it. 'It's in there. It stays in there. We don't react. But if it happens again — wham — the lawyer gets a call.'

'I can't believe she did it.'

'Okay,' he said, 'just this once, she gets the benefit of the doubt. This once. She got a little carried away on Easter, deeply religious woman that she is, and couldn't help herself.' He turned to walk into the living room. 'But next time? Whammo! I don't want to talk about her any more.'

'Don't worry.'

'The hours in our lives we've wasted talking about that woman!' Shaking his head, he seated himself on the sofa. 'Forget about hours. Weeks.'

'I thought we weren't talking about her any more.'

'Months.'

'Benjamin.'

'Years!'

'Don't talk about her.'

'I'm not.'

'So may we move on?'

'I've moved on.'

'Good. Because I called Goya Lewis this morning, as you suggested.'

'Did she give you a name?

'Yes. But she said he would probably advise us to put them back in school and then open a negotiation.'

Benjamin shook his head.

'He's up in Dobbs Ferry.'

'No negotiating . . .'

Elaine walked to a large window at the front of the room.

'I thought you were going to ask for the name of the one who got Garth out of jail that time.'

'No,' she said, 'after we talked about clouds for half an hour she gave me a name from a directory and we said goodbye.'

'Clouds?' he said.

'Clouds.'

'How could you talk about clouds for half an hour?'

'They hold the answer to all our problems,' she said, 'if we know how to

40

interpret them correctly.'

'Elaine, you're the one who brought up the damn lawyer idea.'

'And I'm sorry I did,' she said, looking out the window, 'but unless you want me to call her back and get the name of a cloud in our area, I won't again. Although I don't think it would hurt to call the Dobbs Ferry number.'

'No.'

'Why not?'

'Because we don't negotiate, Elaine. Jesus.'

It was quiet as Elaine watched a neighbor stop his car in front of his garage across the street, get out and push up the door, then get back in the car and drive in. 'I thought the Rigneys had one of those remote things.'

'What?'

'Ted just got out and opened their garage door. I thought they had one of those new remote-control things.'

'How would I know?'

'I thought you talked to him about it once.'

'Elaine, I cannot be thinking right now about whether the Rigneys have one of those new remote-control things.'

'He just opened his garage manually. Maybe it's broken.' She watched Ted Rigney come out of his garage, walk along the front of his house and go inside. 'How do those things work anyway?'

'Elaine, will you please focus on our lives? Instead of the neighbor's latest gadget?'

'These passing fads,' Elaine said. 'They never seem to end.'

'Okay, a gift for Jason and Matt on their birthdays,' Benjamin said. 'A gift for each of them at Christmas. One phone call a year, on her birthday, not to exceed fifteen minutes. Isn't it fully clear to the woman that we moved three thousand miles to get away from her?'

'We moved here because I inherited Dad's house.'

'Which is located here because he moved three thousand miles to get away from her.'

'I'm glad we've stopped talking about her.' Elaine watched Ted Rigney come out of his front door with a small tool kit. 'I was right,' she said.

'About what?'

'It's broken.'

'What is?'

'Ted's thing.'

'Elaine, could you come away from there if it's distracting you?'

'I thought I had window permission.'

Benjamin shook his head. 'There is one thing I will say for that woman — she has not lost her talent for setting us off against each other.'

'But she's well contained. So stop bringing her up. God, I'm sorry I told you about the present.'

She watched Ted roll up his garage door again.

'By the way,' Benjamin said, 'I've had a breakthrough on the school problem.'

'If it has the word "cabin" in it I don't want to hear it.'

'It has the word "motel" in it. If we don't come up with anything better, we'll move into a nice, clean, hygienic, spotless motel up there and use it as a base.'

She watched Ted remove a screwdriver from his tool kit and step inside the garage.

'A base for what?'

'To look around at nice, clean, hygienic, spotless rentals in the area.'

'Benjamin,' she said, looking upwards, 'for the last time, repeat after me — we are not moving to Vermont.'

Ted came back out of the garage holding a metal object in his hand so he could see it better in the daylight. After examining it a few moments, he crouched down and began banging it on the driveway.

'Benjamin, come look at Ted.'

'I don't want to look at Ted.'

'Come look. It'll get your mind off your

43

troubles.'

Benjamin got up from the sofa and joined her at the window.

'The man's cracking up.'

They watched as Ted continued raising his arm and slamming the device down on his driveway.

'Doesn't that cheer you up?'

'It's Step Three of the owner's repair manual,' Benjamin said. ' "If a malfunction occurs, turn bright red and smash product repeatedly against an asphalt surface." '

'This remote-control stuff,' Elaine said. 'I'll be glad when that one passes.'

But the improvement in Benjamin's spirits abandoned him again later in the afternoon, when a call came in from Principal Claymore's secretary.

'So then you or your wife will phone me no later than tomorrow to set up a time to bring the children up to school to meet their new teachers,' the secretary said toward the end of the call.

There was no answer from Benjamin.

'Mr Braddock, I just want to make sure we understand that clearly.'

'We?' Benjamin said.

'I'm sorry?'

'You want to make sure we understand it?'

'That's right.'

'I understand it,' Benjamin said. 'I'm unable to speak for you.'

'I'll expect to hear from you tomorrow, Mr Braddock.'

The phone mounted on the kitchen wall was the one Benjamin had been speaking on. It had a long cord that stretched, so the receiver could be taken into adjoining rooms, and for a long time after hanging up, Benjamin stood looking at the twisted cord as it dangled toward the floor.

Elaine had been sitting at the kitchen table during the call. 'They want to set up a meeting?'

'The four of us.'

'At the school?'

Benjamin nodded.

'What for?'

'Meet their teachers.'

'Who are they going to be?'

'Their names? I didn't ask.'

Elaine looked down at the yellow Formica surface of the kitchen table. She scraped a tiny bit of something from it with her fingernail.

'You know the part of this shit I really can't stomach?'

45

'Try to calm down, Benjamin.'

'Shall I tell you what it is?'

'I already know.' She was rubbing her finger over the spot where she had removed the tiny piece of food.

'You don't know.'

'I do.'

'What then?'

'There's a way you get. It used to happen when we were submitting our petitions. It's always the same thing coming.'

'And what's that?'

'Claymore's sex life.' She looked up at him. 'Right?'

He took a step toward her. 'Okay, I will tell you what pisses me off more than anything else about this whole goddamn thing . . .' He pointed toward the wall. 'That smug, self-satisfied Claymore sitting up there yesterday — that pompous phony telling me how to educate my own children — and you know that self-righteous bastard has fucked everything wearing a dress between here and White Plains, Elaine.'

'Let's have some wine.' She got up and opened one of the cupboards.

'Some philandering, womanizing married person telling me how to raise my own kids, for Christ's sake? I'm supposed to stomach that?'

'Red or white?'

He looked at her as she studied the two bottles on the shelf. 'Elaine, every time there's a crisis I've noticed you have one of two solutions. Either a lawyer or a glass of wine.'

'Red,' she said, taking down a bottle. 'It goes with pissed off.'

'The man is a goddamn creep and you know it.'

She took down two glasses. 'Who cares?'

'Who cares, you say? Who cares that the person telling us we're not fit to educate our own children has had his prick in everything between here and Yonkers?'

'I thought it was White Plains,' she said, pulling out the cork.

'Since I said that he finished off everyone in the other direction.'

She set the glasses on the table and filled each with wine.

'I mean, he has this mousey little nitwit wife. It's not that I blame him. But at least divorce her first if you're supposed to be a pillar of the community and you want to start playing around.'

'Anyway, it's just rumors,' Elaine said, holding his glass out to him.

'You are so wrong, Elaine.' He took it. 'So wrong. When there's that much smoke, you

and stayed there a long time watching Elaine sleep. Then he stood, gathering the clothes up and carrying them downstairs to put on.

As he walked the four blocks of Willard Avenue between his house and the town, the moon was so bright it was like the middle of day, with everything washed white in the moonlight. He looked up at the windows of the houses he passed, the names coming to mind of his neighbors sleeping within.

No one else was on the main street as Benjamin passed the closed shops, finally stopping at a pizza parlor and stepping into a telephone booth on the sidewalk. He reached into his pocket for a dime. As he put the coin into the slot he could clearly see the telephone by the moonlight, without closing the door to turn on the light. He dialled.

'May I help you?' the operator said.

'Yes, I want to call California. And can you charge that to my home number?'

'I can do that for you, sir,' she said. 'What are the two numbers?'

Benjamin stood holding the receiver to his ear, looking at the wall of the booth several inches from his face.

'Sir?' she said. 'The numbers?'

50

He hung up the phone and stepped back outside. In the restaurant he could see the pizza oven with the aluminum trays stacked up beside it. He heard the hoot of an owl, turned to look for it across the street, but there was only the tightly shut bank. At last he went back into the booth. He scooped his dime out of the coin-return tray and re-inserted it into the slot. 'I can't be doing this,' he said as he dialled the operator again.

Benjamin told the boys about the gift from their grandmother the next morning. They were gathered in Jason's room, with Jason standing in front of the others preparing to give a report. 'First of all,' he said, 'I can't just start in with Robespierre. I have to go a little bit into the Revolution first, otherwise you wouldn't see how he comes into it.'

Elaine nodded.

'A present came from California yesterday,' Benjamin said.

The others turned to look at him.

After a few more moments, during which no one spoke, Benjamin said, 'The family policy is no secrets, and that's been on your mother's and my conscience.' He glanced at Elaine. Her head was turned toward him and she was frowning slightly. 'Go ahead with the report, Jason. I just wanted to mention that.'

'A present for us?' Matt said.

'It is,' Benjamin said. 'But let's learn about Robespierre now.'

'Not from California.'

Benjamin nodded.

'But she's not allowed to send us anything again till Matt's birthday,' Jason said.

'We can discuss it after Robespierre.'

'Excuse me,' Elaine said, 'I need to see your father alone.'

'Where is it?' Matt said, getting up from his chair. 'I'll get it.'

'Living-room closet,' Benjamin said. 'Under some stuff in the back.'

Matt hurried out of the room.

'Can we go in our bedroom for a minute?' Elaine said, standing.

'We can't.'

'I'd like us to.'

'After Robespierre.'

'Is it an Easter present or something?' Jason said.

'It is.'

There was the sound of Matt's shoes as he climbed back up the wooden stairs and a moment later he came into the room holding the brown paper-wrapped package. 'She did a bad drawing of a rabbit on it,' he said.

'Let's see.' Jason took it from him.

'I get to open it,' Matt said. 'I brought it up.'

Jason looked for a moment at the rabbit drawn in green marker, then pulled the string off the package to drop in his wastebasket.

'Jason! I brought it upstairs.'

'What difference does it make who opens it?'

'Then let me.'

'It's slippers,' Benjamin said.

Jason looked up from the package.

'A pair for each of you.'

Jason held it out to his brother. 'You can open it.'

'Too late, my friend.'

Elaine stepped across the room and took the package. 'Isn't this the day the new magazines come into the drugstore?' she said. 'Why don't the two of you go down and have a look at those and we'll have the Robespierre report later.'

'I think Robespierre first,' Benjamin said.

'Robespierre later.' Elaine removed Jason's jacket from the end of his bed to hold out to him.

'We'll see you when you get back.'

When they had left the room, Benjamin seated himself on Jason's bed. He waited till he heard the front door shut behind them and then looked up at his wife, who was standing across the room looking back at him.

'Speak,' she said.

'I'm choosing my words.'

'I hope you choose them well.'

Again it was quiet.

'How long do you plan to spend choosing them?'

'They're chosen.'

'May I hear them?'

'You may.'

Several more seconds passed.

'When?'

Benjamin got up from the bed. 'I've decided what to do about the school crisis. It came to me last night. I hope and pray it's the right thing, but at least now we have a plan and we can start taking it forward. In fact it's already set in motion.'

'Set in motion?'

He nodded.

'Already?'

'Yes.'

'What is there about that expression that's not making me feel relaxed?'

'Set in motion?'

'And already. Why am I suddenly experiencing the urge to move to Vermont?'

'I have no idea,' he said.

'You don't.'

'None.'

She looked down at the package she was holding. 'How did you know what this was?'

He shrugged.

'You opened it and wrapped it up again?'

'No.'

She quickly pulled off the brown-paper wrapping. Inside were two cardboard boxes. She removed the top of one and reached in to hold up a slipper.

'A slipper,' he said.

'You did open it.'

'No.' Benjamin looked at his watch.

'Did you take it up to White Plains General and have it X-rayed?'

'Elaine, we need to go get something on Central Avenue. We'll talk about it on the way over.'

'No. We talk about it now.' She returned the slipper to the box, put the top back on and looked up at him.

'You want me to tell you how I knew it was slippers.'

'That's what I want you to do.'

For a long time their eyes stayed fixed together.

'When I tell you,' Benjamin said, 'I need you to be supportive.'

She nodded.

'You will be.'

'If the next words out of your mouth are how you knew what it was without opening it, I will do my best to be supportive.'

'I talked to her.'

'Talked to who?'

Again it was quiet. Then finally Elaine began shaking her head.

'Okay Elaine,' he said, getting up from the bed and taking a step toward her. 'I told you how I knew. Now we need to go to Central Avenue.'

'You called her?'

He looked at his watch again. 'I want to get over there and back so Jason can do Robespierre.' He went out into the hallway.

'Benjamin.'

'Are you coming?' he said, stopping as he got to the top of the stairs.

There was only silence from Jason's room.

'Elaine?'

'Do you remember the sound of me screaming, Benjamin?'

'Screaming.'

'You haven't heard it for a while. I wondered if you remembered it.'

'Let me think back.'

'In ten seconds you won't have to think back.'

He turned around and walked quickly

56

back to the doorway of Jason's room. 'Okay. Now there was something about being supportive, and even though I can't precisely remember the exact sound of screaming, as I do recall it was not a sound that would fall under the heading of supportive.'

'Benjamin, she's the one person in the world we cannot afford to have in our lives again!'

For a long time it was perfectly quiet, till finally Benjamin cleared his throat. 'There's one thing worse than that, Elaine, which is Jason and Matt being back in school in eight days. And I'm asking you to please trust me now, if you ever have. Please. I want a chance to explain, that's all I want. And this may not even be something that will work. But I did not know what else to do, Elaine. Elaine, I did not know what else to do.'

'Are you saying Mother's going to save us from the school board or something?'

'Elaine.'

'Answer me.'

'We need something on Central Avenue, Elaine. I'll answer on the way.'

'What do we need?'

'Equipment.'

'What kind of equipment?'

He reached into his pocket for the car keys. 'Elaine, the clock is ticking and I am going out to the car now and I will explain everything to you on the way over there and now I am going out to the car and I will wait five minutes out there for you to try and compose yourself but then I am leaving for Central Avenue because the clock is ticking and I hope you will be riding over there with me so I can explain everything to you on the way.' He turned around and walked out of the room down the stairs and out to the front and got into their car parked in the driveway.

Four and a half minutes later she joined him.

They didn't talk right away, and in fact they had driven out of Hastings and were on the road leading across the county toward Central Avenue before Elaine finally said, 'When exactly did you talk to her?'

'Early,' he said. 'Three.'

'This morning?'

'Three-thirty.'

'Were you whispering?'

'What?'

'I didn't hear you.'

'I didn't call from home.'

'Where did you call from?'

'Town.'

She turned to look at him.

'The phone booth by the pizza place.'

'You walked to town at three in the morning?'

'God, Elaine, there was this totally full moon. It was completely eerie.'

'Benjamin.'

'It was so bright you could see your shadow on the sidewalk like it was the middle of the day. Really.'

She reached over to turn the car key.

'What are you doing?'

She removed the key from the ignition switch. Benjamin put both hands on the wheel as the power steering cut off and maneuvered the car over onto the shoulder of the road as it slowed. When it had come to a stop he twisted his head around to look out the window as a car whizzed past a few feet away. 'Elaine.'

'Could we start over, please, omitting the lighting conditions?'

'Sure. But if I talk a little faster than usual it's because we're both going to be dead in two minutes.'

Elaine turned to look through the rear window as a car hurtled past them, honking its horn. She reached over, returning the key into the switch. There was a loud scraping noise as the engine started again. 'Drive over farther and stop.' She kept her hand

on the key as Benjamin drove over the
shoulder and across a grassy space. She
turned the key and pulled it from the ignition switch. 'Finish what you were saying,'
she said, 'and this time hold the moonlight.'

The car rolled forward and stopped beside
a large wire enclosure. It was filled with
dogs. Another large pen was behind the first
one and then another. The dogs in the nearest cage ran over to put their paws up
against the wire and bark loudly at the car.

'This is where you want to chat?'

'Everything, Benjamin. Every word you
said. Every word she said.'

Benjamin looked at a Doberman pinscher
growling at them from the other side of the
wire.

'Let's see. Okay. Well she was asleep.'

'Go on.'

'I apologized for waking her up.'

'Go on.'

'Are you going to say "go on" after each
sentence?'

'Go on.'

'She more or less collected herself. She
looked to see what time it was. She was
taken aback by the call, obviously, but after
collecting herself she said what a wonderful
surprise it was to hear from me. I said it
was nice to hear her voice too.'

A tiny white dog beside the Doberman was yapping and leaping wildly up and down.

'May I suggest a new venue?' Benjamin said.

'Go on.'

'Go on speaking or go on to a new venue?'

'Speaking.'

'She asked if the boys got their slippers. I said they had. She asked if they liked them. I said they did. She asked if they were the right size. I said they were a perfect fit.'

'Go on.'

'Elaine, I am "going on" quite spontaneously, without the need to be prodded after every third word.'

'Go on.'

'She apologized for sending the present. She said she knew it was wrong and she had agonized over it and she just couldn't help herself. She said she often cries herself to sleep thinking about how the boys are growing up without her being part of their lives and she knew she shouldn't send the gift but there was a void in her life and she was powerless to stop herself.'

On the other side of the crisscrossed wire of the cage, a cocker spaniel was standing quietly among all the other gyrating, bark-

61

ing dogs and wagging its tail as it looked at them.

'Look at that one,' Benjamin said.

'Crying herself to sleep. Void in her life. Go on.'

'She asked how you were. I said you were fine and busy. She asked if you were happy because that was the most important thing to her in the whole world.'

The cocker spaniel took a step forward as Benjamin continued looking back at it. 'I'd like to get that one,' Benjamin said.

'My happiness the most important thing in the world to her. Go on.'

'She said it was the greatest tragedy of her life that her thoughtless behavior had made it so the precious childhood years of Matt and Jason's life were passing by without her being able to share her love with them.'

'How long did that shit go on?'

'About two minutes. That was the main theme.' He pointed at the cocker spaniel, still looking at the car and wagging its tail. 'I'd like to buy that one.'

She glanced at the dogs.

'That one,' he said.

'I know which one.'

'May I?'

'No.'

'But it loves me.'

'What else?'

'She's checking into the Ardsley Motel next Wednesday.'

A new dog came to the end of the cage, pushing in between the others and putting its foot into a water dish as it began howling at them.

Elaine's eyes turned down to the dashboard.

'She won't be calling us. She won't be coming to see us. There will be no contact with her whatsoever and she understands that.'

Elaine turned to look at him and it was quiet. 'What?' she said finally.

'No contact. No phone calls. All of which she fully understands.'

Again it was quiet except for the barking.

'Mother is coming to the Ardsley Motel?'

'She is.'

'Wednesday?'

'I appreciate that it's a hard concept to grasp.'

'Mother is coming to the Ardsley Motel, five miles away from our house?'

'Nine or ten, I think.'

Again it was quiet.

'But not three thousand.'

'I don't think the Ardsley Motel is quite three thousand miles from our house, no.'

Elaine looked back through the windshield at the pens. On the highway an occasional car whizzed past. 'Benjamin, I had this terrible nightmare last night. It was ghastly. Let's see how it went — oh. We were going to Central Avenue and we pulled over next to all these dogs going crazy in these cages and you told me Mother was checking into the Ardsley Motel next Wednesday.'

'May I have the car key?'

'It was so real. You were saying all these strange things about its being bright sunlight in the middle of the night and Mother telling you on the phone how much she loved everybody.'

He held out his hand.

'But then I woke up. God. I've never been so relieved in my life to find out it was only a nightmare.'

'The key please, Elaine.'

'You were asking me for a key in the dream. The barking dogs, the key. All the symbolism — Freud would have gone crazy.'

'I need to go to Radio Shack, Elaine.'

'Why?'

'For the equipment.'

'What equipment is at Radio Shack?'

'Electronic.' He opened her fingers and removed the key. 'And I will tell you what the electronic equipment is,' he said, insert-

64

ing the key into the ignition switch, 'which will be your next question, on the way there.'

'Tell me now.'

'And that's the last question till we're on our way again?'

'Yes.'

'We need two tape recorders.'

She looked down at the door of the glove compartment. 'Two tape recorders,' she said.

'A small one. And one we can make duplicate tapes on.'

She nodded. 'And why do we need those?'

'When we're on our way over, Elaine.'

As he turned on the engine a man in knee-high boots was coming along a concrete walkway toward the nearest dog pen. The cocker spaniel turned to look at him, wagging its tail even harder than before as h approached.

'Fickle,' Benjamin said as they bump over the shoulder and onto the high again. 'At least you still love me.'

'Let me get back to you on that.'

When they returned home from ( Avenue, Benjamin called Principa more's secretary and set up a me the following morning, which the said was a good day because it w

day of Spring Recess and the teachers would be in and out of the school, finishing up paperwork, and the boys' new teachers would not only be able to meet the children, but Benjamin and Elaine as well, which was also an important part of the process of re-bonding with the school.

When the four of them arrived next morning at Principal Claymore's office, Ms Friedman and Ms Cummings were there, and they each told Benjamin and Elaine how exciting it was what they had tried to do with Matt and Jason, and the idea of home education was a truly intriguing one, and at some point there would probably be a way to structure things so that dedicated parents like the Braddocks, who wanted to participate more fully in their children's learning experience, would be able to coordinate with the school, and perhaps have the children home for an hour or two a week if there were an effective way to monitor them and if a way could be found so that the other pupils and their parents weren't confused by the innovation.

Seated at his desk, Principal Claymore removed a pen from his jacket pocket as the teachers spoke, taking notes and nodding as he wrote down what they were saying. Then Matt and Jason paired off with their teach-

ers and went to see their new classrooms.

'Those are two dandy teachers,' Principal Claymore said, 'on that you have my personal guarantee.'

'I could sense their dedication,' Benjamin said.

His wife glanced at him.

'Make yourselves at home, folks.' The principal indicated two chairs facing his desk.

'Thank you.' Benjamin seated himself in the chair beside the one Elaine was taking.

'End of semester.' Principal Claymore held up his arms. 'Boy oh boy! But you two remember what that's like, from before.'

'Do we ever,' Benjamin said.

Again Elaine glanced at him.

'Okay now.' The principal rolled his chair up to his desk. 'First of all I want to say that I admire so darn much what you two were trying to do with your boys — all of us here at Warren G. Harding do — and I don't think I got this across properly at our meeting the other day, Ben, but if every parent had the kind of concern and caring you two have for your kids it would make our jobs a walk in the park.' He looked at Elaine. 'A walk in the park,' he repeated.

She nodded.

'And as I told your other half before, those

two boys are going to bring back into our little community all that nurturing help you've been giving them during their absence and it's just going to spread out through the other pupils in a warm glow.'

Benjamin nodded. 'I hope so.'

'Don't just hope so. Because it is. Gloria and Susan and I were just speaking before you came about the incredibly enriching influence Matt and Jason are going to have on the rest of us.'

'Excuse me,' Elaine said, 'but aren't there some practical matters we came here to discuss?'

'All business,' Benjamin said, gesturing at her.

'These women, Ben.' Principal Claymore leaned toward Benjamin and put his hand up beside his mouth. 'They don't let the grass grow under our feet, do they?'

Benjamin laughed as Elaine said something under her breath.

'Sorry?' Principal Claymore said, turning to her.

'Nothing.'

'I missed that.'

'She said she thought there's been a change in the school-bus schedule since the boys were here before,' Benjamin said.

'Oh yes.' The principal pulled open a

drawer of his desk. 'And I should have' —
he began rummaging through it — 'a schedule right here. If I can ever . . .' He looked
up long enough to give Benjamin a wink.
'This drawer's beginning to look like my
wife's purse.'

Elaine's nostrils flared slightly as Benjamin chuckled again.

'Ah.' The principal pulled up a leaflet to
hand across the desk to Elaine.

'Thank you.'

'And there's a brand-new fleet of buses
since the boys were here. That's another
treat for them to look forward to.'

Matt was carrying a printed sheet of paper
when he and Jason came back to the office.
'A parent has to sign this,' he said, 'so I can
visit the bird sanctuary.'

Principal Claymore removed the pen from
the vest pocket and held it out toward
Matt's parents. 'If one of you can just put
your John Hancock on that I'll see it gets in
the right pigeonhole.'

'We'll look at it at home first,' Elaine said.

'I'll do it,' Benjamin said, taking the pen.
Matt gave him the form. He set it on the
desk to sign at the bottom.

'Thank you, my good man,' Principal
Claymore said as he took it. 'Oh. Before I
forget.' He returned the pen to his pocket.

'That crazy staff baseball game we have every Spring Recess is coming up in a few days. Have you folks ever taken that in?'

'We haven't,' Benjamin said. 'It sounds interesting.'

Jason glanced at his father.

'Our staff plays the high-school staff. It's a heck of a lot of fun and nobody much gives a darn who wins, that's the best part.'

'Can anyone come and watch?' Benjamin said.

'Come one, come all. We'd love to see you.' He winked at Elaine. 'I'll hit a home run with your name on it.'

'You get a nice turnout, do you?' Benjamin said.

'Always. Parents come. Pupils from both schools love it.' He aimed a wink in Matt's direction. 'The kids all come to watch their teachers make fools of themselves.'

'Oh listen,' Benjamin said, 'I think we're squared away now about getting everybody back in school, but if we do have any questions over the break — I can't see that we will — but I guess there's no way to get in touch with you till school starts up again.'

The pen came out of the pocket again. 'Ben. Now come on. I'm there for my people. Kids. Staff. Parents. Night or day. Break or no break. I'm there. That's the kind of principal I try to be.' He wrote down a number to hand Benjamin.

'I'm sure we won't need it, but it's re-assuring to have.'

'An ear to listen and a hand to help,' the principal said. 'That's me.'

After asking Elaine to drive home, Benjamin got into the back seat with Jason, and when he had closed his door tilted his head back and began sucking in large gulps of air.

The others turned to look at him.

'Are you all right?' Elaine said.

He placed his hand on his chest. 'Fine. Just drive home.' He took three more deep breaths and then several quick short ones.

'Are you having a panic attack or something?' Elaine said.

'No. Let's go.'

She started the car, glancing in the rear-view mirror at him as she drove slowly through the parking lot. 'Are you really . . . ?'

'I'm all right. Just drive.'

She turned out of the lot and into the street. Benjamin removed his hand from his chest and his breathing slowly returned to normal.

'Hey Dad,' Jason said after they'd driven for several blocks, 'could I ask you a personal question?'

'Shoot.'

'Was it my imagination back there, or were you kissing Principal Claymore's ass?'

'Your imagination.'

'Oh right,' Matt said, twisting around in the passenger seat to look at his father. 'I thought your lips were going to stick to the guy's sphincter by the time we got out of there.'

Elaine opened her mouth to say something, but after a moment or two closed it again and silently drove them home.

Elaine didn't want to talk on the tape recording of instructions that was to be waiting at the motel when her mother arrived. She was lying on her back on their bed as Benjamin made the recording, rewinding the tape and going over what he had said again and again till he felt sure all the complicated instructions were clear. 'God,' he said when he was done. 'Finally. Now a word or two from you.'

'I don't want my voice on there.'

'Just a word or two.'

She was looking up at the ceiling. 'Why am I letting this happen?' she said.

'Because, for the trillionth time, you don't have a better idea.'

She lifted her head up slightly from the

pillow and looked over toward him. 'Hello, Mother.'

'Well wait till I turn it on, could you?' Benjamin turned on the recorder again and motioned for her to speak.

'I don't want my voice on it.'

'Shit, Elaine.' He turned it off and rewound it again, then played the tape forward to erase her words. 'Okay, now when I turn it on, just say "Hello, Mother" again.'

'No.'

'You already said it once.'

'Right. And I will not say hello twice to that woman.' She raised herself up onto her elbows. 'You do realize we can go to prison for this.'

'Who can?'

'We, Benjamin.'

'What charge?'

'Has blackmail not crossed your mind?'

He shook his head. 'Unless you extort money, it's not technically blackmail.'

'Really?'

'Really.'

'And you know that?'

'I do.'

'How do you know it?'

'My father was a lawyer.'

'And he told you that?'

'No. But you get a sense of these things if

you grow up in a lawyer's household.'

'I grew up in one too,' she said, 'in case I haven't mentioned it.'

Benjamin pushed the tape recorder a little ways away on the table, then moved a school yearbook in front of himself and opened it, looking down at the large photo of the smiling face that filled the page.

'Benjamin?'

'What?'

'Why didn't I get a sense it wasn't blackmail in my lawyer's household?'

Benjamin closed his eyes. 'Elaine,' he said, quietly and slowly, 'if you have a better plan, please tell me what it is. Otherwise, just . . . just . . .'

'Butt out.'

'Well put.'

'I'll look on the bright side,' she said, resting her head back on the pillow. 'With Sing Sing right up the river, it's only an hour's train ride for Matt and Jason to come visit on Sundays.'

Benjamin took hold of the yearbook page with the large face on it and carefully tore it out. 'Are you going to speak on the tape or not?'

'I shall speak.'

He picked up the tape recorder. 'Wait about three seconds after I turn it on.' He aimed it in her direction, then turned it on.

Elaine waited three seconds. 'Hello, Mother.'

'Jesus!' He turned it off.

'Now what did I do wrong?'

'You said it with a snarl.'

'I want it with a snarl.'

Benjamin looked at the machine a few moments, then nodded, 'You're right.' He pressed the rewind button. 'The snarl's good. She shouldn't feel overly welcome.'

He folded the photograph in half and picked up a large rubber band from the table.

'Let's see the picture again.'

He opened it and held it up.

'God,' she said after looking at it for a few moments. 'If ever there was a match made in hell.'

He fastened the photograph to the tape recorder with the rubber band. 'She'll know how to work this thing, won't she?'

'Yes, Benjamin.'

He opened a cardboard box on the table containing several layers of bubble wrap and placed the machine inside, then rested several loose cassettes on the player before closing the lid. He took a wide roll of tape, pulled a length from it and sealed the box. 'Can you look up the zip code for Ardsley?'

And she did.

The Braddock family occupied seats on the top row of bleachers across the field from the bench where the players sat when their team was at bat. Behind the players' bench was a high wire fence, and behind the fence a parking lot. And at just two-thirty a blue car drove into the lot, then drove slowly along a row of parked cars and turned into a parking space at the end.

Elaine glanced over Matt's head at Benjamin, but his gaze was fixed on the car that had just arrived. Elaine looked back at it again to see her mother step out, standing beside the vehicle a few moments and looking around. 'Jesus help us,' she said in a whisper.

'What?' Matt said.

She shook her head.

Matt turned to look at his father, who had placed his hand on his chest. Benjamin slowly drew in two deep breaths.

'Dad, you okay?'

'Fine. How about you?'

'Fine.'

'What's the score?' Benjamin said.

'It's up on the board.'

Jason had gone to a refreshment stand at the end of the bleachers, and as his grandmother found her way between parked cars and toward the tall wire fence he paid the girl behind the counter and picked up a cardboard container that held the refreshments. As he carried it along the edge of the field his grandmother reached the fence, stopping to look through the wire at the playing area. As Jason reached the steps leading back up to their seats, he glanced out across the field, took the first step, and then stopped.

He stood there several seconds, looking down at the refreshments he was holding, then put his foot back down on the previous step and turned back toward the field. Benjamin, who had been watching him, got to his feet. 'I'll go help Jason.'

'He can manage, Dad.'

'He's forgotten where we are.'

Matt stood and began waving his arm. 'Jason! Up here!'

Elaine pulled him back down onto the wooden seat.

When Benjamin got to him Jason remained standing where he had been before, frowning down at the concrete step in front of him.

'Everything okay?'

'Dad,' he said, looking up at his father.

Benjamin reached out for the cardboard holder. 'Let me take these.'

Some Coke splashed out of a tall cup as Jason pulled it back. 'Dad, wait a minute.'

'They're waiting for us.'

'But I have to tell you something. You won't believe this.' He turned toward the field again. 'I can't believe it myself.'

'Tell me back at the seats, Jason.'

'Look over there, Dad. By the fence. Look who's there. I swear to God you won't believe your eyes.'

Benjamin removed the holder from his son's grasp, then took one of his hands. 'We're blocking people's view,' he said, leading him up the stairs.

'Dad, I'm sure it's her. You've got to listen to what I'm saying.'

'We'll talk about it at the seats.'

A cheer went up from a group of people near them.

'Dad, stop.' He pulled his hand away and pointed across the field. 'It is. It's her.'

Benjamin took his son's hand again, pulling him to the top and then leading him along past the other spectators in their row.

'Is my hot dog still hot?' Matt was standing, waiting for them.

'You aren't going to believe what I'm going to tell you,' Jason said.

'Just tell me if my hot dog's still hot.' Matt removed his hot dog from the container as

80

his father seated himself beside him.

'This is something more incredible than anything that's ever happened.'

'Sit down, Jason,' his mother said.

'God, this isn't even hot any more, Jason.'

'It never was hot. Please listen to me.'

Benjamin took a napkin from the holder and dried off the sides of the large paper cup of Coke. 'You two were going to share this, right?'

'Please look where I'm pointing!'

Wearing a red coat, a scarf and dark glasses, the woman was walking along the other side of the fence. She reached an opening and walked through it, stopping to look at the players seated on the bench several yards away.

'Matt,' Jason said, 'tell me you can see her too!'

Matt took a bite of his hot dog, chewing it as he looked across the field. 'What's she doing here?' he said.

Reaching across the others to take Jason's arm, Elaine pulled him down onto the bench. Benjamin handed him his hot dog. 'Eat this before it gets cold.'

'I've got news for you,' Matt said.

On the other side of the field, the woman in the red coat had taken a step closer to the players seated on the bench, then stopped to watch the game.

'She shouldn't be back there if she's not on one of the teams,' Matt said.

'Mom,' Jason said, leaning forward to look at his mother, 'am I crazy or is everybody else crazy?'

'Everybody else. But we'll talk about it when we get home.'

Wearing a pair of shorts, a T-shirt with broad stripes and a baseball cap, Principal Claymore was crouched slightly, several feet away from the bag that was third base, and when the pitcher, who was the janitor at Warren G. Harding, threw a final strike past the drama teacher from Franklin High, the principal hooted, tossed his baseball glove up in the air, caught it as it came down and walked off the field as the players that had been seated on the bench got up to take their positions.

Principal Claymore seated himself at the end of the bench and, when all the members of the high school team were in place, one of the math teachers from Franklin pitched the ball to the elementary school nurse and she hit it back to him, a loud cheer rising from the bleachers as he caught it. Then the math instructor pitched the ball to the fourth-grade teacher from Warren G. Harding but it went behind her.

Jason had begun shaking his head. 'I'm sorry, people. Forgive me, people. But I cannot wait till we're home to talk about this.'

The woman had come to stand at the end of the bench, bending down to say something to Principal Claymore, whose head was twisted around so he could listen to her.

Jason's arm shot out as he pointed to them. 'Look now!'

'What would those two have to be talking about?' Matt said.

Benjamin pushed his son's arm down.

'You're wrong, Mom,' Jason said. 'I'm the one who's nuts and everybody else is totally sane.'

Elaine reached over to rest her hand on his knee. 'Jason, she's back here to see if it might work out for a visit. But we aren't going to see her immediately, if at all.'

'You knew she was coming?'

'We thought she might be.'

'Well, where's she staying?'

'In Ardsley,' his mother said, 'and if it doesn't work out to see her without disruption, then she'll just go back home. But I really don't want to keep talking about it now.'

Principal Claymore had stood so he wouldn't have to crane his neck around to talk to her.

'All right, Jason?' Elaine said.

He shook his head. 'I mean it might be nice to be told about these things once in a while.'

Benjamin handed him the cup of Coke. 'Jason, we should have told you, and both of us owe you an apology. But it's a very tense time for the family right now, and we want you to forgive us.'

Principal Claymore had to interrupt his conversation with their grandmother to take his turn at bat, but he quickly struck out. She was standing back by the fence when he returned, and he joined her there to continue their conversation.

A sixth-grade teacher from the elementary school came to the plate next and hit the ball into center field. But Mr Mouser, the Franklin gym coach, caught it and threw to second base for a double play that retired the sides.

Once again the staff members from the two schools changed places on the field, but as play resumed the sound of a loud and scratchy voice came over the public address system. *I have an important announcement, everybody. We have a line-up change for Warren G. Harding. For the rest of the game, Ruth Crandall, school nutritionist, will be taking the*

84

*place of Principal Claymore at third base.*

Benjamin watched as the blue car stopped at the edge of the parking lot. One of its signal lights began blinking, then it turned out onto the highway.

The instructional tape had been delivered to the motel on Tuesday so that it would be waiting for Elaine's mother when she checked in on Wednesday. The baseball game was held the following day, and the plan was that if she was successful, Elaine's mother was to send her own tape back to them Friday by special delivery, so that it would arrive overnight, two days before the boys were to be back in class on Monday morning.

In fact the postman did bring the tape Saturday morning, and after Benjamin had signed for it he took it to the car to play it in the cassette player under the dashboard, since he didn't want it to be overheard in the house. As he listened he kept shaking his head and repeating 'Jesus Christ' over and over, but after only seven or eight minutes he turned it off and took the cassette up to his and Elaine's bedroom. After locking the door (even though there was a strict family policy against locking doors), he brought out the larger tape recorder he had bought on Central Avenue and made several copies of the original cassette, continuing to take the Lord's name in vain every few minutes.

Benjamin kept waking up all through the night and every few hours he roused Elaine to tell her he couldn't go through with it. Her response was always the same, which was to say, 'So don't', and then go back to sleep. One time he asked her to tell him what he should say when he confronted the principal, but by the time he had finished asking the question she was asleep again.

He still hadn't decided on the speech, even after the meeting had been set up by phone on Sunday morning, and though he always found particularly unconvincing the scenes in films where the hero is rehearsing out loud to himself difficult things he is preparing to say, that is exactly what Benjamin found himself doing as he slowly circled the block on which the principal lived. 'Principal Claymore,' he said, gesturing with his free hand, 'for reasons known only to yourself and Superintendent Anello, you've chosen to provoke a showdown with my family. You know as well as I do that no parents came to you with complaints. I guess you decided it was too much nuisance for you to go on the way we were, and you gave us the axe. Well, Principal, this may come as a shock . . . I know I appear a mild-mannered fellow, but with my back to the wall I can hit below the belt as hard as you can. Harder in fact. And even though this is by far the grubbiest, most sordid situation I've ever found myself in . . .'

They'd agreed by phone that Principal Claymore would come out and talk to Benjamin in his car for a few minutes, and so after pulling into the driveway, stopping when he got to the closed garage door, Benjamin gave a little toot on his horn. In less than a minute the front door of the house opened and Principal Claymore came out onto the porch and walked across the grass to Benjamin's car.

'Ben,' he said, opening the passenger door and getting in, 'as I told you the other day, I'm always there for parents, but I do need to say that these breaks are when Doris and I get to spend a little quality time together, so I hope we can resolve whatever you have on your mind without taking up any more time than we have to.'

'We can,' Benjamin said, nodding. 'We can definitely resolve it in a short time.' He put his hands on the steering wheel. It was quiet as he studied the wedding band on one of his fingers.

'Something about your boys going back tomorrow?' the principal said. 'Some wrinkle you want me to help iron out?'

'It is about that.' Benjamin had stopped nodding, but began again. 'The . . . the boys going back.'

'What is it? Everything's on track as far as I can see.'

Benjamin turned to look at him. But instead of speaking, he pursed his lips and slowly drew in a deep breath. It whistled slightly as it passed between his nearly closed lips.

The principal frowned.

Benjamin tipped his head back slightly, letting his mouth fall open so that the next intake of air occurred soundlessly.

'You okay, Ben?'

He nodded, taking several sharp but shallow breaths.

'Do you need a doctor?'

Benjamin shook his head.

'You sure?'

'I don't.'

The principal watched as Benjamin blew in and out several times and then took an extremely deep breath.

'Here's what let's do, Ben,' the principal said, reaching for the handle of his door. 'I'll go back inside. You sit out here and think about things for a few minutes. And if there's something you still want to talk about, just give a little honk and I'll come back out.' He pushed the handle down to open the door beside him, then put his foot out onto the driveway.

'Wait.' Benjamin reached toward one of the buttons of the cassette player under the dashboard. He placed his finger on the button, and then again the two of them sat silently beside each other for a few seconds.

'I'm going in now, Ben.' He turned to put his other leg out of the car.

Benjamin pushed in the button and suddenly Principal Claymore's voice came loudly out of a speaker on the dashboard.

*Oh look at those pretty pink nipples.* There were several moments of silence. *May I touch your pretty pink nipples with my pee-pee?*

Benjamin's breathing had stopped altogether. He pushed the button in again and the recorded voice stopped.

Sitting beside Benjamin, staring through the windshield at the door of his garage, Principal Claymore remained motionless.

Finally Benjamin pressed a second button. A cassette popped partially out of a slot below his hand and he removed it. 'Here,' he said, holding it in front of the principal.

The principal stared down at it.

'Sir, I did not know what else to do. But I am so sorry.'

The other man turned to gape at Benjamin.

'Sir, I am so, so sorry.'

The principal's lips parted slightly but he didn't speak.

'Oh my God, sir, you just should have left us alone.'

The man's lips began moving but it wasn't till after several seconds had passed that any sound came out of his mouth. 'More?' he said finally, his voice sounding differently from the last time he had spoken.

'What?'

'More copies?'

Benjamin nodded. 'Yes. More copies.'

Suddenly they turned to look at the house as the front door opened and Doris Claymore stepped out onto the porch. 'Ralph?' she called toward Benjamin's car. 'Don't you and Mr Braddock want to come inside to talk?'

The principal grabbed the tape out of Benjamin's hand and got the rest of the way out of the car. Benjamin watched as the man hurried around the front of his car, pushing the cassette down into the back pocket of his pants, then walking quickly across the lawn toward his wife, laughing and calling something to her that Benjamin couldn't understand.

On Monday morning Jason started a new project, on the history of medieval armor, and in the afternoon Elaine quizzed Matt on the geography of North and South America.

Benjamin made sure that at no time during the day was he out of hearing range of either the upstairs or downstairs telephone.

But neither of them ever rang.

# Two

When the two of them arrived at the motel coffee shop, Nan had already found them a table, and as they came through the entrance she rose, opening her arms as they approached and then wrapping an arm around each of them, holding them tightly against herself for several seconds before releasing them to step back saying, 'My God but the two of you look terrific.'

Elaine nodded. 'Mother.'

Benjamin glanced at the table beside them. 'So, Nan. You found us a table.'

'And I promise I won't embarrass you by saying it again,' she said, returning to her chair, 'but I really have never in my life seen either of you looking as relaxed and happy as you look at this moment. Sit. Sit.' When they had taken the chairs opposite hers she reached across to take Benjamin's hand in one of hers and Elaine's in the other, then sat looking at them with a wide smile.

95

'You look good,' Benjamin said finally.
'Doesn't she? Tan?'

'You do, Mother. Wonderful.'

'You're both so sweet.' She let go of their hands and picked up a menu from the table. 'I'm so excited I don't think I'll be able to eat anything.'

'Just coffee for me,' Elaine said.

'Same,' Benjamin said.

Nan looked over at a waitress behind the counter, nodding for her to come to the table.

'The first thing Elaine and I need to say,' Benjamin said as the girl started toward them, 'is how very very much we appreciate that you . . . that you . . .'

'What you did for us,' Elaine said.

'Oh darling, you know I'd walk over burning coals for those two little sweethearts.' The waitress was standing beside the table with her pad. 'Now,' Nan said, 'why don't we all have something silly like a piece of cake?'

'Fine,' Benjamin said.

'Elaine?' her mother said.

'Piece of cake — sure.'

'Do you have chocolate?' Nan said, looking up at the girl.

'Belgian chocolate.'

'Three pieces of Belgian chocolate —

whatever the hell that is — and three coffees.'

The girl walked away.

'Ben,' Nan said, 'in case I don't say it again, I just have to tell you how absolutely thrilled I was the other night when you called to say Nan could do something to help her little angels.'

'It was a good way to get back in touch.'

'Thrilled to the core.' She opened her purse, then looked up at her daughter. 'Dear, I know how you feel about my smoking . . .'

'Go ahead.'

'Ben?'

'Go ahead.'

'But he was so mysterious,' she said, removing a package of cigarettes from her purse, then lowering her voice. ' "There's something we want you to do and if you go to such-and-such a motel, a tape will be waiting for you with instructions." I mean, I was just sure you were going to have me bump someone off.' She shook a cigarette part way out of the pack, putting the end of it between her lips to pull the rest of the way out. 'And then when I got here,' she said, reaching into her purse for a lighter . . . 'the management had left the package in on my bed, and when I got here . . .' She lit the cigarette and dropped the lighter back in

97

her purse. 'When I got here and as I was sitting there listening to it — Elaine, I was sure I'd stepped right into an episode of "Mission Impossible".'

Elaine reached across the table to pat her mother's hand. 'Mom, we know what an unusual thing it was to ask. But the boys are still at home, thanks to you, and their education is proceeding in the way that's best for them.'

'Ben, just slide that ashtray over here, can you?'

'We'll never forget how you came through for the four of us at this crucial time,' he said, pushing it across the table to her.

'My God, can I bring this off?' I mean, that's the first thing I said after listening to the tape. 'Walk up to this man I've never seen before in my life, in the middle of a baseball game, and cart him off to bed?'

'Let's see,' Elaine said, frowning slightly, 'I'm just trying to think. The boys have their schedules. But seeing you is what they're most excited about right now.'

'Oh, and by the way, Ben, I didn't follow the suggestion to tell your principal I was looking for clerical work in the area. When I got to the game, that just didn't seem . . . I don't know . . . it didn't seem me, really, so I did depart from your script on that point.'

She took a drag from her cigarette. 'I said I was passing through on my way to a funeral up in Maine — of a very distant relative, I didn't want him to think I was too grief-stricken — and I was looking for something to do after checking into my motel for the night, and I saw the game in progress and wondered if it would be all right to watch it for a while.' She blew a stream of smoke over their heads. 'Well, the man offered me a sightseeing tour of the area even before I'd finished my little spiel, and as God is my witness we were between the sheets in less than forty-five minutes.'

The waitress appeared beside the table holding a tray. The three of them were quiet, watching her set a small plate of cake and a cup of coffee in front of each of them.

'What we were thinking,' Benjamin said, picking up his fork as the girl walked away, 'to give you a feeling of how home education differs from the traditional school model, is why not come over tomorrow and sit in on one of our —'

'But a weirdo?' Nan fitted her cigarette into an indentation in the ashtray, then shook her head. 'I'm sorry, but unless you'd sent along that picture from the school yearbook there is no way you could have convinced me that man was an elementary school principal. Ben, I really don't think he should be working with children.'

Benjamin took a bite of cake.

'For one thing he could not keep his penis out of my armpit.'

Benjamin coughed, spraying small bits of cake out onto the table, as Elaine glanced at the people at the next table. 'Mother.'

'Well he was,' she said. 'A total weirdo.'

'Okay. But I think we've talked about it enough.'

'Now listen to me, darling,' Nan said, reaching across the table to put her hand on her daughter's arm. 'You know how terribly much I've wanted to help your little family for so long in whatever way I possibly could. And I was thrilled to tears to be given this opportunity. But dear, let's face it, it was not your usual favor from a doting grandmother — far above and beyond the call of duty, as Ben so eloquently put it on his tape — so I'm not going to pretend I wasn't traumatized by the experience. Because whatever else you may think of me, dragging strange men away from sporting events and into bed isn't something I've done before.'

'Well actually,' Elaine said as her mother removed her hand from her arm, 'that isn't exactly true.'

'What isn't true, darling?'

'I'm thinking of . . . what's his name.'

'What's whose name?'

'The British one.'

'Oh yes.' Nan frowned for a moment. 'Wasn't his name Nigel?'

'You found him at a sporting event. He owned a horse running at Santa Anita. After the race you went up and complimented him on his jockey's outfit.'

Benjamin raised his hand slightly.

'Wasn't he the one who suggested the boys call me Nan?' Nan said. 'Before that you two had them calling me something flattering like Granny Robinson.'

'We're getting sidetracked,' Benjamin said.

'But I guess I have made an exception about dragging strange men away from sporting events if they're a Lord, haven't I,' Nan said.

Elaine looked up at the ceiling.

'Well he was one, darling. He showed me his papers.'

'Those were his horse's papers, Mother.'

'Yes, and it said Lord Nigel on them. After Owner.'

'No, Mother. It said Lord Nigel after Horse.'

Nan glanced at Benjamin. 'God, she has me sleeping with his horse now.'

'Let this go,' Benjamin said, turning to his wife.

'I mean personally, Elaine, I don't give a shit if he was the King.'

The people at the next table stood, and began picking up their plates to move.

'Well, maybe the King,' Nan said.

'Let it go!' Benjamin said, as Elaine again prepared to speak.

She looked down at the glass of water beside her plate. She studied it for several seconds, then took a deep breath. 'All right, Mother, he was a Lord. But don't you think we've heard enough about what went on with Principal Claymore in the motel room now?'

She shrugged. 'I just thought you'd be interested.'

Benjamin picked up his napkin. 'We have an opportunity here,' he said, beginning to clean flecks of chocolate cake from the surface of the table. 'The three of us. An opportunity for a new start. Let's not throw it away.'

His mother-in-law cut herself a bite of cake. 'Hear hear,' she said, raising it to her mouth. 'And let's begin our new start by you both telling me every last little thing my two sweet darling precious angels have been up to all this time their Nan's been

102

kept away from them.'

A basic tenet of Benjamin and Elaine's home-schooling philosophy was that nothing fell outside the boundaries of education — life itself was education — and when anything came up in the course of events that was a source of interest it was incorporated into the matrix of ongoing learning. Such an opportunity for intellectual growth presented itself the next day.

It was the end of the afternoon and the four of them were standing on the front porch as Nan climbed into the taxi she had insisted on calling to save them the trouble of driving her back to the motel. They watched as she closed the door, then leaned forward to say something to the driver.

'Isn't there an expression that goes something like, "Subtle as a train wreck"?' Jason said.

Nan rolled down the car window and threw them kisses as the taxi backed into the street.

'Jason,' Elaine said as the others waved at the departing taxi, 'once in a great while someone comes along who makes us appreciate train wrecks.'

Benjamin held open the front door for the others to go in ahead of him.

'So are we going to fix up the room in the basement?' Matt said.

Elaine glanced at her watch. 'Five bloody hours.'

'Mom?' Matt said.

'No, we're not.'

'She thinks we are.'

'She can think what she wants.'

'God,' Jason said, 'I mean, why can't she just say, "I want you to fix up the room down here for me to stay in when I visit." Instead of like, "Oh, when Jason goes off to college — if any will take him — he's going to want to bring a friend home on weekends and wouldn't it be fun to turn this into a little guest room?" '

'Sometimes Nan doesn't say exactly what she means,' Benjamin said.

'Ben,' Elaine said, 'the light's still on down there. Can you get it?'

Benjamin went back down the stairs to the basement, then stood a few moments in the doorway of the small storage room.

It had remained just as it was five years ago when Elaine's father had died. Several large cardboard boxes were stacked against a wall, a table turned upside down on the cement floor beside them, and in the corner a pile of furniture partially covered by a dusty sheet. A grimy sink protruded from

104

one of the cinder block walls, in which there was a flower pot filled with dirt but no plant.

He clicked off the light and returned up the stairs. 'I think we need to come up with a project of some sort to study devious behavior,' he said, entering the kitchen before noticing no one else was in the room. He went into the living room, which was also empty. 'Where is everybody?' He stood a few moments looking at one of the walls. 'God,' he said finally. 'I've just thought of the perfect project.' He started up the stairs. 'Listen to this.'

Elaine was lying on her back on their bed, her eyes closed and her hand resting on her forehead.

'Elaine, listen to this. What if every day we each thought of a lie to tell the other family members? During the course of the day we'll each just slip a little falsehood into the stream of conversation, then in the evening we'll sit down and see which of the others can figure out what it was. To see who's the most perceptive.'

She continued lying there, the back of her hand on her forehead.

'As a way of studying devious behavior.'

She remained motionless.

'Elaine?'

'What?'

'Did you hear what I said?'

She nodded once, but said nothing more.

He watched her a few moments. 'I guess you're wiped out from the visit.'

She made no response.

'Right. Well why don't you lie down for a while?'

Matt was at his desk with his face buried in his arms, which were folded on the blotter in front of him.

'Matt, I've had sort of an interesting idea for a project I'd like to run past you . . .'

Matt spoke without lifting his head. 'I'm waiting for a couple aspirins to kick in, Dad,' he said into his arms. 'Could I get a rain check?'

Benjamin went down the hall to his other son's room. Jason was also lying on his bed, but on his stomach, his hand hanging down and resting on the floor. 'Right,' Benjamin said. He stepped back into the hall and closed the door.

The plan was for the four of them to drive over the next morning and meet Nan at her motel so they could sit and talk in her room, but as they got ready to leave, Goya Lewis called from Vermont to find out what had happened about the school deadline (rather than go into it, Elaine just told her they seemed to have dropped the demand), but in fact it was fortunate the motel trip was delayed by the call because otherwise they would have missed the decorator, who came while Elaine was still upstairs on the phone.

Matt was looking out the living-room window when Melody's car pulled up in front and parked. He watched as she came up the walk, then opened the door for her as she stepped onto the porch.

'Hello,' she said, putting her hands on her knees and bending forward slightly toward him, 'I'll bet you're one of those two little angels I've been hearing about.'

'I am.'

'Is the family here now?' she said.

'It is.'

'And may I come in?'

'You may.' Matt went back into the house and she followed him.

Jason was coming down the stairs.

'I'll bet you're the other little angel,' she said.

'I didn't catch your name,' Matt said.

'Melody Francis.'

Jason stopped at the bottom of the stairs to look at her.

'And are your mother and father here?'

'Could I ask what it's about?' Jason said.

'I'm going to turn that old basement stor-

107

age room of yours into a pretty little guest room.'

It was quiet a moment, then she pointed back and forth between them. 'Shouldn't you two be in school?'

'We're home taught,' Jason said.

She frowned. 'Home taught.'

'As opposed to school taught.'

'What does that mean?'

'Our parents teach us.'

'Can they do that?' Melody said.

'They seem to think so,' Matt said, looking up as his father came down the stairs.

'Mr Braddock. I'm Melody Francis.' Melody smiled as she held out her hand for Benjamin to shake. 'Your mother-in-law probably told you I was coming.'

'Not that I recall.'

She let go of his hand and looked past him to Elaine, who was coming down the stairs next.

'Mrs Braddock? Melody Francis. Your mother told me the exciting plans you have for your basement room.'

'She what?'

'The conversion.'

'Conversion?'

'You want to convert it into an exquisite little guest room.'

It was quiet a moment, then Elaine shook

108

her head. 'Oh no.'

'Well, I've just been on the phone with her for an hour.'

Elaine walked past her and to the front door. 'There were some mixed signals between me and my mother.'

'You're not renovating it?'

Elaine opened the door for her. 'My mother was mistaken.'

It was quiet a moment, then Melody reached into her purse. 'I see. Well let me give you one of these,' she said, taking out a card, 'in case you change your —'

'We won't.'

She continued looking at Elaine, who stood with her hand on the knob of the open door, looking back at her.

'Here,' Benjamin said, stepping forward to take the card.

'So I guess it's goodbye for the moment,' Melody said.

'For the moment and more,' Elaine said.

Melody went to the door, stopping a moment to look back at them, then going out as Elaine closed the door after her.

'How come you took her card,' Jason said to his father, 'if there's no chance of hiring her?'

'Because she looked like she was going to cry.'

'Somebody is going to cry,' Elaine said, picking up the car keys from a table. 'Come on. I want to get this over with.'

As it turned out, Elaine's words were in fact prophetic; but ironically her mother's tears weren't a source of satisfaction to her, as Elaine had anticipated, but rather, it could be said, had the opposite effect.

The five of them had been sitting in the motel room for half an hour or so when Nan suddenly got to her feet without explanation and walked quickly into the bathroom. She partially closed the door, and then it was quiet, the others remaining seated where they were as they waited for her return.

Finally Matt made a gesture toward the bathroom. His father shrugged.

Jason, who was seated on the bed beside his brother, leaned forward slightly so he could see partway into the next room. 'You okay, Nan?'

There was no answer.

After a few more moments Benjamin said, 'Everything all right in there, Nan?'

When she finally did emerge she was holding a box of tissues. She removed one of them as she crossed the room to seat herself in her chair. The others watched as she touched the corner of one of her eyes, shaking her head. 'Oh boys,' she said, 'I am so sorry for you to see your nan like this.'

'Mother . . .' Elaine said.

'No no.' She raised her hand to silence her daughter.

'I'd like to rephrase what I said.'

'I think the point Elaine was trying to make,' Benjamin said, 'was that —'

'No Ben,' his mother-in-law said, dabbing at the other eye, 'I appreciate that you're trying to play the peacemaker. But Elaine was raised to speak her mind and she needs to say just what she's thinking.' She glanced over at Matt and Jason, sitting side by side on her bed. 'It's just that for my precious angels to see their nan this way makes me feel so terribly embarrassed.'

'It's okay,' Matt said.

She turned to smile at her daughter. 'You can rephrase it, darling, if it's important to you.'

'Mother,' Elaine said very slowly, 'you have my deepest and most heartfelt apologies for calling you manipulative, but I really think Benjamin's suggestion is the best compromise. After you leave we'll go ahead and have the storage room renovated, and at Christmas time you can come for a few days for a visit.'

Nan frowned at her. 'Darling, you make it sound as though we're in a business meeting — talking about "compromises". We're all family here, dear.'

'But what about my suggestion?' Benjamin said.

Nan shrugged. 'I thought it was fine.'

'So shall we plan to do it that way?'

'But you know, Ben, it would just be so much fun if I could be here to watch it take shape. An experience of a lifetime for me. It really would be.' She pulled up a new tissue from the box. 'Not to get in the way. Just to take a taxi over for a few minutes every other day or so to see how it's coming along.'

They watched her blow her nose.

'But for us,' Benjamin said, 'the fun would be watching your reaction when you came back at Christmas and saw it all finished.'

'Don't you have stuff you have to do back in Los Angeles?'

'Oh yes, Jason darling, Nan has a wonderfully exciting life back there. Between daytime TV and my AA meetings there just aren't enough hours in the day.' She touched her eye again.

Elaine turned to her husband. 'Give me the decorator's card.'

Raising himself up from his chair slightly,

Benjamin removed it from his back pocket and handed it to her. Elaine sat down beside Matt on the bed and picked up the receiver of the phone. 'Do you have to dial an outside line first?'

'Nine first,' her mother said.

The others watched as Elaine dialled the number on the card, waited a few moments, then spoke. 'Is this' — she looked back at the card — 'Melody Francis?' She nodded. 'You were at our house earlier this morning about turning the . . .' She nodded. 'Right. Okay, I realize you didn't look at the room itself, but based on what my mother told you, and that we'll do all the cleaning up and painting the walls ourselves . . .'

Nan raised her hand to interrupt. 'Darling, you're not to worry about the cost.'

'I wasn't, Mother.'

'Oh, it sounded like you were.'

'Generally speaking,' Elaine said into the phone, 'how long do you estimate it will take to do the job? Putting in the fan and getting the sink in working order are the only major things we can't do.' She nodded. 'Thank you.' She hung up.

'How long?' Benjamin said.

'She'll have to get back to us.'

'Darling,' her mother said, 'you also need to put in a toilet down there.'

'There's one off the kitchen.'

'Well, I know, dear, but you need one down there too, simply to increase the appraisal value of your house, if nothing else.'

'I have an idea,' Jason said. 'What if we put one in ourselves? We always do carpentry stuff, but never any plumbing.' He looked at his father. 'There was a plumbing store we passed on the way over. We could check it out on the way home.'

'Ben,' his mother-in-law said, smiling for the first time, 'what a creative suggestion from Jason. I hope you'll let me take back every criticism I've ever made of this home-schooling idea of yours.'

'Of both of ours.'

'I'm sorry?'

'It was Elaine's and my idea together.'

'Matt and Jason are so spontaneous and inventive I'm just . . .' she shook her head. '. . . I'm just, I don't know what. What a super-terrific job you're doing with these boys of yours, Ben.'

Elaine stood. 'Let's go.'

'So soon?'

'So we can stop at the plumbing store and get things moving.'

The others got to their feet as Elaine, saying something under her breath, walked across the room.

'What, darling?'

She shook her head.

'We couldn't hear what you said.'

'Nothing, Mother.'

Elaine went to the door as Benjamin, Jason and Matt joined her.

'Dear, it's rude to talk to ourselves when we're in company.'

'Just one of those irrelevant thoughts that come into your head at odd times for no reason and aren't worth repeating.'

'But you've got us curious,' her mother said.

'I'm curious,' Matt said.

'It was a short-story title.'

'You don't write short stories, dear.'

'I know. It's totally irrelevant.'

'What's the title?' Jason said.

'Grandma's New Potty,' Elaine said, opening the door so the others could walk out past her. She looked back at her mother. 'See? It really wasn't worth repeating.'

'You're right, darling, it wasn't.'


The event that had precipitated the enforced separation of the boys from their grandmother had occurred seven years earlier, when all of them were residents of southern California. Nan had stopped by their house to pick up the very young children for a shopping trip to nearby stores one afternoon, as she occasionally did during that period of their lives, and then the three of them had disappeared.

An hour had been stipulated for the trip's duration, and so as evening approached, Benjamin and Elaine had become frantic. The police were called, along with everyone Elaine could think of that her mother knew (these included friends whom her mother had been out of touch with for years, whom Elaine remembered from childhood, one of whom didn't even remember who Elaine and her mother were), but it wasn't till late the following afternoon, after a long and sleepless night and another desperate day, that finally a phone call had come through from Jason, announcing that they had all decided to fly up to San Francisco and belatedly celebrate his birthday, which had taken place the month before.

Their parents were on the next flight to San Francisco themselves, after the management of the St Francis Hotel had been notified they were coming. The police in that city had also been notified (although they felt Benjamin and Elaine were greatly overreacting to an impromptu junket by two boys with their grandmother) and Jason and Matt were retrieved in the lobby of the hotel

116

to fly back home with their parents. After that incident, the relationship with Elaine's mother, which had been strained as it was, had permanently changed.

There were no actions directly involving the courts, but lawyers were brought into it, and made it clear to the boys' grandmother that to forestall the taking out of a restraining order, any further contact with her grandchildren would have to occur under whatever conditions her daughter and son-in-law chose to impose on her.

Of course, the remorse of Elaine's mother was boundless, and she even attributed stopping drinking alcohol to the 'wake-up call' the event had been for her (although when applauding herself for this salutary step she invariably failed to mention that continued heavy alcohol use would be the one factor the attorneys told her would give her daughter and son-in-law the power to revoke the limited agreement altogether — and, for what it's worth, it might also be inserted here that the attorneys involved in putting together this arrangement were, coincidentally, from the very firm with which her late husband had been associated for so many years).

Nan's tearful entreaties, on the infrequent phone calls that were permitted following her San Francisco adventure, were not persuasive in cajoling Elaine and Benjamin into overturning the agreement and, after it had been in place for two years while they all lived in southern California, Mr Robinson passed away and left his house on the Hudson River to his daughter, who, with great relief, joined with her husband even before the will was out of probate in making plans to relocate to the other side of the country. Nan's last in-person contact with the family, prior to the current visit, had taken place five years before at Los Angeles International Airport, where she had bid them a moist and heartrending farewell under the watchful gaze of an attorney who at Elaine's invitation was standing on the other side of the Departure Lounge.

And so, with this background in mind, it wasn't surprising that the boys' parents were, to say the least, mildly apprehensive on the following afternoon when Nan took her grandchildren in a taxi up the Hudson River to the town of Irvington, named after the author Washington Irving, and boasting the home of that renowned writer himself (this choice of an outing followed the proposal of a train trip with her grandchildren into New York City for a shopping spree, a suggestion that had been emphatically vetoed). And so, as a result of much begging (and more tears, it should be noted), and despite two earlier visits by the Braddock family to the historical literary site, this attraction became, one afternoon, the destination of Nan and her two precious angels.

The parents of the two angels spent the afternoon occupying themselves with various tasks — straightening the hall closet, cleaning the oven — as they waited for the agreed hour of four o'clock to arrive, at which time, if they had not yet returned, questions would have to be raised about the 'new era of trust' Nan had repeatedly proclaimed they all were embarking upon.

Several trips down to the basement were also made as they waited, and it was on one of these that Benjamin proposed an 'insurance policy' he had in mind in case matters threatened to get further out of hand than they already had since Nan's arrival.

In the former storage room, several paint cans were resting on the floor and there was a small pile of dirt and nails and bits of wood in the center of the room. Benjamin took a broom leaning against the wall and swept around the edges of the pile, neatening it, as Elaine watched.

'I really am insisting the plumber be here

119

to supervise when you and Jason put in the toilet,' she said.

He shook his head.

'I really am, Benjamin.'

'You might be insisting,' he said, 'but I'm not going to defeat the whole purpose by having some twenty-dollar-an-hour —'

'Benjamin, I'm not going to argue about it.'

He rested the broom against the wall again. 'We promised not to let her turn us against each other.'

'It's not turning us against each other to make sure the basement isn't transformed into a lake.'

The flowerpot had been removed from the basin, which had been cleaned out and scrubbed. Elaine stepped over to it and turned the handle of the tap. There was some sputtering, then water blasted out into the sink.

'He said not to use that yet,' Benjamin said.

'I'm not using it.'

'He said not to turn it on.'

She turned it off and looked over at a bed, tipped up against the wall, the mattress still wrapped in a sheet of plastic. 'The basin and toilet will take up half the room,' Elaine said. 'What we're going to have is a bathroom with a bed in it.'

'Let me tell you my insurance-policy idea,' Benjamin said.

'Your what?'

'Insurance policy,' he said. 'Okay. Now, let's say she doesn't show any signs of leaving, even after the room's finished. Knowing her, you have to consider that contingency.'

'Don't worry.'

'So here's what we do.'

Elaine leaned back slightly against the edge of the sink.

'I wouldn't do that till it's reinforced,' he said.

'It's steady.' She folded her arms across her chest. 'What's the insurance policy?'

'Okay, first we tell Jason and Matt what happened between Claymore and your mother.'

'Benjamin.'

He held up his hand. 'Hear me out, Elaine. We come up with a palatable way of putting it to them. Airbrush it, obviously.'

Suddenly there was a loud scraping noise and Elaine threw her arms forward to keep her balance.

'We can approach it on a birds and bees basis,' Benjamin said.

Elaine turned around to look at the sink,

tilted sideways on the wall. 'We've done birds and bees.'

He shrugged. 'I don't know — maybe we use it as a way of getting into the subject of recreational sex . . .'

She bent forward to straighten up the sink. 'Benjamin, when they start dating, I don't want it in their minds that a good time is putting it in the girl's armpit.'

'That's what we airbrush.'

She turned around and leaned back against the sink again. 'So how is it an insurance policy?'

'Okay, no details for them, but we get across that the two of them had sex. Then, if worse comes to worse, and your mother thinks it might be nice to extend her stay, we tell her that they know about it.'

Elaine frowned.

'Which will totally alter the dynamic of her relationship with them.'

'How?'

'Don't you see? If she's aware they have that image of her, she'll be so uncomfortable around them she'll be out of here like a shot. Aversion therapy. Every time she sees them she'll feel shame.'

'Shame.'

'Right.'

'My mother will feel shame?'

'In front of her own grandchildren she will, yes.'

'What planet did you say you were from?'

Elaine lurched forward again as the back of the sink scraped down along the wall.

A taxi drove up in front of the house just at four o'clock and deposited the two boys. Nan chose to remain in the car and throw kisses as it carried her off to Ardsley.

'She bought herself this huge headless-horseman statue in the gift shop,' Jason said as they came inside.

'She's going to put it on her television set at home,' Matt said, 'so she'll think of us every time she watches TV.'

Benjamin closed the door after them.

'And by the way,' Matt said as they started up the stairs to their rooms, 'we found out what Nan and Principal Claymore were talking about that day at the baseball game.'

'Oh?' Benjamin said.

'Matt asked her,' Jason said.

'And what did she say?' Elaine said.

'She told us she knew how important honesty was in our family and she wanted to enter into that spirit with us.'

They stopped at the top of the stairs.

'And?' Benjamin said.

'And she told us what happened with

123

him,' Jason said.

It was quiet as the two of them looked down at their parents.

'Go on,' Elaine said.

Matt glanced at his brother, then back down the stairs. 'It's a little shocking, Mom. I'll need to think of a nice way to put it.'

Sometimes, although always in a tentative way, taking care never to do it with the heavy hand of authority, Benjamin introduced topics of study to his sons in which it was he who felt the primary interest — rather than allowing their own natural curiosity to guide them — in hopes his excitement would spill over. Occasionally this seemed to work, although usually it didn't, and then he would quickly abandon the project. One subject that had proved particularly deadly was based on a book the library had once acquired about the gods of ancient Greece. After looking through it when it came in, and finding the subject intriguing, Benjamin had taken it home to pass around at the dinner table, but aside from a few perfunctory comments it was clear the deeds and adventures of these mythical beings held a fascination only for himself, and when he went to work the following day he returned the book to the library shelf.

But what originally sparked Benjamin's interest, as he had leafed through the book, was the notion of the Greeks believing in gods and goddesses who delighted in playing tricks on the very mortals who revered them.

It fascinated Benjamin to think about a system of deities for whom those who worshipped them were an object of sport and amusement, often cruel, and following an event that took place a week after Nan had arrived in Westchester County it crossed his mind that the Greeks might have had it right about the whimsical nature of the gods.

The call came in the afternoon. Elaine answered the phone in the bedroom.

'Is that you, Elaine?' the man's voice said.

'Yes.'

'I'm Walter Healy. Do you remember me?'

There was a pause. 'Mother's neighbor?'

'In the house next to hers,' he said. 'She gave us her key before she flew back to see you all, and we've been keeping an eye on the place.'

'I see.'

There was another pause.

'Is she handy, Elaine?'

'Well she's not actually staying with us. Is something wrong?'

125

'Elaine, the Van Noordstrom's house, there on the property behind your mom, burned to the ground last night.'

'Oh no.'

'It burned to the ground not ten hours ago, Elaine.'

'No.'

'Thank God Millie and Tom got out.'

'Thank God.'

Frowning slightly, Benjamin stepped into the bedroom. 'Who's . . .'

She motioned for him to be quiet.

'I need to talk to your mom, Elaine.'

'Of course. Well, is her house okay?'

'It happened at two in the morning — Fran woke up and saw orange light playing on our bedroom wall through the window. Then the minute she got me up and we figured out what was happening, I ran over to Mom's back yard and turned on her hose and wet everything down. She lost that big palm tree at the back of her property, Elaine, but that was all.'

'Really?'

'Just tell me who it is,' Benjamin said.

Again Elaine motioned for him to be quiet. 'Well, let's see,' she said. 'So the Van Noordstroms are okay?'

'Thank the Lord for that.'

'Do they know how it started?'

126

'They think — well they know — it was a leak on a propane tank Tom bought yesterday for their motor home. They keep it there in their garage, you know, so people won't see it from the street, and he said he thought the tank smelled funny when he put it on.'

Benjamin left the room to go downstairs.

'I can't imagine they could sell one of those tanks that wasn't a hundred percent safe. But then in the middle of the night it just went boom. I talked to Millie again not more than an hour ago. Boom!'

There was a click as Benjamin picked up the phone downstairs.

'Well, you can imagine what Millie and Tom are like at this point.'

'Sure.'

'Boom! And then a minute or two later the place was engulfed. Millie said she had time to grab the family photo album and a necklace and Tom got hold of a few of their stock certificates and out they ran onto the front dichondra in their bare feet.'

'Incredible.'

'Fran and I are completely traumatized of course.'

'Of course.'

'I'm on the other extension,' Benjamin said. 'It sounds like there was a fire.'

'Ben, as I stand here speaking to you the

127

house in back of Elaine's mom's is a pile of blackened rubble with a chimney sticking up — like you see on the news.'

'Terrible.'

'Yesterday at this time a beautiful, beautiful home stood there and now there's just a chimney rising up where that beautiful sunken living room of theirs used to be.' He paused for a moment. 'Elaine, how can I get hold of Mom?'

'Do we want to upset her about this right now?' Benjamin said.

'Well, she'll have to extend her stay back there,' Walter said.

There was a pause of several seconds.

'You said her house is fine.'

'Elaine, Mom's dining room looks right out on that sickening blackened ruin. And the hell of it is the damn county won't let them bulldoze the rubble away until they've sent out a fire team to do an inspection, whenever that will be. I really don't think Mom can handle sitting there eating her dinner in the evening and looking out at that, do you?'

'Maybe she could close the curtains,' Benjamin said.

'How do I contact her?'

'Let me think,' Elaine said.

'By the way, why isn't she staying there

with you folks?'

'Listen,' Benjamin said, 'wouldn't it be better for her to come back home so you break it to her in person? To ease the blow?'

'Oh no, Ben, she needs to know ahead of time, so she can prepare herself. But boy aren't we lucky she's back there with family so you folks can help her through this. How do I reach her?'

As Benjamin and Elaine expected she might, Nan found news of the fire so distressing that she was unable to remain by herself in the motel, and since, at that point, the new guest room was nearly finished, she moved into it later that same day.

Unsupervised by a member of the plumbing profession, Jason and his father had installed the new toilet that very morning, although for some inexplicable reason sheets of water ran down the wall behind the tank every time it was flushed. Finally Elaine was permitted to call the plumber, who told her to shut off the valve to prevent water entering the tank till he could get out to fix it in a day or two. But as Nan said, after arriving in her taxi, Benjamin carrying her suitcase in through the front door behind her, 'How in the name of God can I complain about walking up a few steps to take a wee after what happened to the Van

129

Noordstroms?'

Down the street from their house was a small park where Jason and Matt often went to throw a baseball back and forth. But on the day the plumber was coming to finish things up — it had taken him more trips than he'd originally intended — it was Benjamin and Elaine who were in the park, where they'd also spent much of the previous day.

They were seated on a bench, and though they'd been there for over an hour, neither had spoken. Benjamin was slouched backwards, his head tipped up and his eyes closed, while his wife sat slumped beside him, supporting her chin on her hands.

At last Benjamin lowered his head and opened his eyes. He sat a few moments looking out across the park, then stood. 'Wait here,' he said.

'Where are you going?'

He started away from the bench.

'You can't tell me where you're going?'

'I'll tell you when I get back.'

'Benjamin,' she said, getting to her feet.

He turned around. 'To make a phone call.'

'To whom?'

'When I get back.'

'Tell me now.'

'When I get back,' he said again.

130

'Now.'

'No,' he said, 'when I get back.'

'Now.'

'Just sit down, Elaine.'

'Don't tell me to sit down.'

'Okay I won't.'

'You'd better not.'

'Seat yourself.'

She watched as he turned around and walked slowly across the park before sitting down again. Then she watched him go into a phone booth to make the call, then as he came out and walked slowly back again.

'Who'd you call?'

He sat down. 'The plumber.'

'Why?'

'To tell him not to come.' He tipped his head back again and closed his eyes.

Elaine looked at a bird that landed on the ground several yards away from them. 'What?' she said as it flew off.

'I'm too exhausted to repeat it. You'll have to retrieve it from your memory bank.'

'You told the plumber not to come?'

'Nice retrieval.'

'Is that right?'

'He's not coming.'

'The plumber's not going to finish up the toilet today?'

'Here's a game,' he said, his eyes remain-

131

ing closed. 'Let's see who can think of the most ways to say the plumber's not coming.'

'Out of this whole nightmare, in which the only thing that's keeping me sane is that at least the toilet you and Jason screwed up, which I knew you would — Benjamin, getting that fixed was the one thing I had to look forward to this whole day!'

'You don't want to build your day around a toilet.'

Elaine looked at a tree beside the bench. 'He cancelled the plumber,' she said to it.

'Let me know when you're ready to hear the reason.'

It was quiet again for a while till finally she turned back to him. 'Benjamin, have we ever been at each other's throats this badly before?'

'No.'

'Well can we stop?'

'I don't know.'

'Well can we try?'

They sat without talking for nearly five minutes, then Elaine said, 'Did I tell you what she said to Matt this morning?'

'You did.'

'About how she's going to contribute to their home education?'

'You told me.'

'She's going to have them watch "General

Hospital" with her every afternoon so they can learn how to be doctors.'

'I don't want the toilet fixed,' Benjamin said, 'because I want her to keep having to come upstairs to piss.'

'That's why you cancelled the plumber?'

'So she has to keep using the one off the kitchen.'

'And you think that's going to make her leave?'

He nodded.

'Benjamin, climbing nine or ten steps to go to the bathroom will be at most a minor inconvenience for her.'

'At the moment.'

The bird landed several yards away, looked at them and flew off again.

'Well, when will it be more than a minor inconvenience?'

'When she has to wait in line behind Garth and Goya and their kids to use it.'

As had become her habit since arriving three days ago, Elaine's mother spent part of the afternoon in the back yard reading, and when they returned home from the park it was there that Elaine found her, on the chaise longue with her book open on her lap.

'Darling?' she said as her daughter stepped

133

out into the yard. 'As long as you're up, can you just run down to my room for my white sweater?'

'Sure, Mom.'

'I'm sure I left it right in sight. Oh and Elaine? Just glance in my purse while you're down there and see if there's a cigarette left in my pack — there may not be.'

Elaine went back in the house, through the kitchen and down the stairs to the new guest room, where the sweater was resting on her mother's bed. The purse was on the table. She rummaged through it, pulling out a small blue envelope and some other papers to look in the bottom. She carried the sweater back up the stairs and through the kitchen and out into the yard.

'I know that was a bother.'

'Not in the least.'

'Cigarettes?'

'None left.'

'Well maybe you or Ben could pick me up a new pack next time you go down. Just put that over my shoulders.' She leaned forward and Elaine fitted the sweater over her mother's shoulders. 'I'm so spoiled by my California weather, I almost didn't think to bring that.'

'Matt needs some help with his spelling,' Elaine said, smoothing the sweater down

134

her mother's back, 'but there's something I should probably mention first.'

'Why don't you sit down, dear?'

'Just for a minute.' Elaine seated herself on the lawn beside her mother's chaise. 'I'm trying to remember — did we mention the Lewis family to you?'

'At dinner last night.'

'Oh that's right.'

'They sound like total barbarians.'

'Oh no.'

'Darling, I'm just going by what you and Ben told me about them.'

'They did meet at Radcliff and Harvard.'

'You mentioned that,' her mother said, 'but that only means they're passing out degrees to barbarians these days.' She looked back at her book. 'For the boys' sake you really do need to start choosing your friends more carefully, dear.'

Elaine reached down to pull up a few blades of grass. 'They were an incredible help to us when we were getting started — their advice. Garth and Goya were really the ones who gave us the confidence to make the break.'

'They've served their purpose for you then.'

Elaine put a blade of grass between her teeth. 'Sometimes Garth likes to come down

135

to the city and use the Law Library.'

'He's a lawyer?'

'No. He studies it on his own.'

Elaine's mother turned a page of her book.

'The library has an extensive Civil Rights section,' Elaine said.

'That's nice for him.'

It was quiet for a few moments.

'Come to think of it,' Elaine said, 'I think they actually might be planning a trip to the area.'

Her mother's eyes moved an inch or two down the page, then stopped. 'What area?'

Keeping her front teeth closed, Elaine yanked at the blade of grass, biting it in half. 'This one.'

Her mother looked over at her.

Elaine turned her head to spit out the small piece of grass.

'Well you won't have to see them, will you?'

She looked back at her mother. 'We probably will, to be honest.'

'Do you know when they're coming?'

'Tomorrow.'

It was quiet a few moments as they looked at each other.

'Tomorrow,' her mother said.

Elaine nodded.

'And you'll be seeing them?'

'We really should.'

'Well I suppose that's your business. But if you must, I will ask you to do me the courtesy of not meeting them here at the house.'

'Where should we meet them?'

'In town. See them somewhere for coffee. Or hyacinth tea, or whatever.'

Elaine looked back at the lawn.

'And I think you'd better let me keep the boys here while you're with them. I really feel strongly about that.'

Elaine picked another blade of grass to put between her teeth.

'Darling, don't keep doing that. Dogs eat grass when they're going to vomit.'

She spat it out. 'I don't see how we can meet them in town.'

'Of course you can.'

'But where will they stay?'

'I'm sorry?'

'They always crash with other home schoolers when they're on the road.'

After a few moments Elaine's mother closed her book, then sat looking down at its title, which was *Rachel's Destiny*. 'Darling, tell me I'm not hearing you correctly.'

'About what?'

'Elaine, don't act stupid with me. I know you too well.'

'Mom, we owe them a huge favor.'

'Not that huge.' She looked back at her. 'You aren't saying this is something that's already arranged, are you?'

'I guess I am.'

'Well how in hell did that happen?'

'What happen?'

'That it got arranged. Did they call? I haven't heard the phone ring all day.'

'Benjamin talked to them when we were out.'

'He called and invited them?'

'The call might have been about other things and in the course of it they might have said they were coming down. I really don't know — I wasn't with him when he talked to them.'

Her mother turned in the chaise so she could put her feet down on the ground. 'Well didn't he tell them I'm here?'

'I didn't hear the call, Mother.'

'So in other words, whenever someone wants to move in with you, you just roll over and say come ahead.'

'Now that you mention it,' Elaine said, looking up at her, 'that does seem to be our pattern.'

Her mother stood. 'Well call them back.'

'What do you mean?'

'I mean call them back and tell them I'm

'Don't m

'But wit

just now -

the two o

my feelin

points me

you.'

Elaine

into the

she said,

'I'm su

of whoe

'Who?

'This

just po

the fam

'I thi

'Althou

'Oh

:kl

ı I

t

here. They can't come now.'

Elaine nodded. 'That would be good.'

'It is good. Do it.'

Elaine removed one of her hands from behind herself, where she'd been bracing herself against the grass, and studied the crisscrossing patterns on her palm.

'Elaine.'

'What?'

'Go call them back.'

'I wish I could.'

'You can.'

'They already will have left by now.'

'To get here tomorrow?'

'They're spending the night with a family in Massachusetts and then get down here at the end of the afternoon tomorrow.'

'I can't believe this is happening.'

'It just sort of came up.'

For a long time Nan stood looking down at her daughter. 'I don't suppose Benjamin happened to ask if their nine-year-old is weaned yet?'

'He's twelve now.'

'And is he weaned?'

'You'd really have to take that up with Aaron.'

Her mother glanced at the elderly woman in the next yard as she picked some wilted flowers from a bush, then looked back at

her daught
Massachus
  'We have
  'Elaine,
enough fo
  'Four.'
  'Four?'
  'They
  'Nefertiti
  'What's
  'Nefert
the day
her yet.'
    'Why
    'She tl
    'Haun
    'She
    'Is thi
    'Oh
and br
want to
    'Dar
less of
think
    'The
    'Ho
    'Th
sleep
  He
darli

because his duties were not demanding and he was free to think his own thoughts as he went about them. When they relocated to Hastings he enquired at the library there and by coincidence one of their employees was preparing to leave. Benjamin applied for his job. And after he had looked over the application, the head librarian there, a man named Raymond, asked him to come in for an interview, leading him into a small reading room when he arrived.

'Shelving,' Raymond said after the two of them had taken their seats. 'That's what you put down as the position you held in California.'

'Shelving. That's correct.'

'And how did that work suit you?'

'Very well.'

The completed application form was resting on Raymond's knee. He studied it a moment before speaking again. 'Because I see here you were educated at one of the Ivy League schools.'

'Attended one,' Benjamin said.

'Attended.'

Benjamin nodded.

'Well, did you finish?'

'I finished.'

'Because you just said attended.'

'I attended it, yes.'

'And graduated.'

'Both.'

'So you were educated there?'

Benjamin didn't make a response.

Raymond looked at him another moment, then back at the form. 'Volumes maintenance director is the position we have opening up,' he said. 'You'd intake and inspect all new acquisitions, cross-cataloguing them before entering them into our inventory. Also under your purview would fall ongoing responsibility for the reintegration of all revolving titles back into the system.'

It was quiet for a few moments.

'What was that title again?' Benjamin said.

'Volumes maintenance director. You'd be referred to as the VMD.'

The two men looked at each other for several seconds.

'Shelving,' Benjamin said finally.

'That's right.'

Elaine's father had invested wisely during his lifetime, and along with his house he left his daughter a portfolio of stocks, the dividends from which provided a reliable, if not lavish, source of income. But it wouldn't have been possible for Benjamin to simply live on his wife's holdings (for one thing, this example wouldn't have been one he could have permitted himself to set for his

143

sons), and so even though the library job wasn't strictly essential, economically, it was necessary for other reasons, and Benjamin had fulfilled his responsibilities as VMD conscientiously and happily since they'd moved to the east coast.

But, even though it brought in their basic living expenses, the library job wasn't something that was viewed by Benjamin as a vocation as such. His vocation, he had come to realize as time went on, was to see if he could prevent what had been done to him by the various institutions he had passed through from being repeated in the case of his offspring.

After their visit to the Lewises in Vermont, Elaine had several times wondered aloud where Garth and Goya's money was coming from, since neither of them was employed, but in the end Benjamin's annoyance with the question — in his mind the force they were for change in a moribund educational system was the only relevant issue between them — caused her to drop the subject, and she imagined one of them probably also had family money, and if it was Goya then clearly Garth's scruples didn't stand in the way of his participating in his wife's wealth as Benjamin's did. But of course the source of their income was

144

the farthest thing from anyone's mind on the night the four of them moved in.

They didn't arrive till nearly one in the morning and, although Elaine's mother was still up, and had been vociferously expressing views on their impending visit similar to the ones she had shared with Elaine in the back yard the day before, when the headlights from their van played across the living-room wall as they turned into the driveway she went quickly down to her room.

Matt and Jason had gone to bed — around eleven-thirty — and as the four Lewises carried their bedding in through the front door, Benjamin apologized that the boys hadn't stayed awake to welcome them but that they wanted to be fresh to spend the following day with them.

Goya and Garth and their two children deposited their things in the living room, each choosing a corner for their own, making a little pile of clothing beside their sleeping bag and air mattress. Then Elaine showed them where the kitchen and the bathroom were, and when finally it was obvious their guests had no interest in going to bed right away, Benjamin made coffee for everyone and took it into the living room, where they sat for a couple of hours

145

conversing on the subject of home education and the obstacles various families were encountering in their respective communities. But a frequent digression, made by Goya and punctuating the more serious subjects at regular intervals, was, 'I keep getting this vibe coming up through the floor. Go tell your mother to come up and meet us.'

'She was just totally exhausted,' Elaine said.

'She's fine,' Benjamin said.

'Up through the floor,' Goya said, moving her hands up and down. 'Like a bad mist rising.'

Garth had been sitting in the corner as his wife had been the one primarily extolling the virtues of home schooling.

'Button it, Goya,' he said.

'Don't you feel it?'

'I think she wanted to get some sleep to be fresh when she met you in the morning,' Benjamin said.

'Is that the official mantra around here?'

'Button it, Goya.'


In the morning Nan took a train into the city and spent the day going in and out of shops on Fifth Avenue, something she had wanted to do since she'd first arrived. And although she had repeatedly tried to talk Jason and Matt's parents into letting the boys come along with her on such a jaunt, the new arrivals prompted her to abandon this effort, and she got up and dressed and left while everyone else was still sleeping, which represented a radical break from her usual routine of rising toward the middle (or even at the end) of the morning; and after breakfast at the coffee shop in town she boarded a train along with a throng of commuters that carried her into New York to the fashionable street, where she found herself drinking coffee for nearly three hours until the shops' doors were opened.

Later in the morning, Garth also took a train into the city, although not to Fifth Avenue, but to the Law Library, where he looked up cases in which governments, companies or other organizations had attempted to coerce individuals into conforming to standards of behavior to which they objected. In particular there was one which attracted his attention entitled 'Macys versus Entwhistle', in which a legal action had been taken by that store against one of its salesmen who refused to wear socks to work, and as he went back and forth through the pages, taking notes on the arguments and ultimate outcome (Macys prevailed), he was heard more than once by a young law student reading in a large book across the table from him to mutter the words, 'You cock-suckers' under his breath.

After a breakfast of some food they had brought with them, Goya and her daughter went out together to get acquainted with the town of Hastings-on-Hudson, while Jason and Matt entertained Aaron. This left Benjamin and Elaine alone for the day, which they spent in bed, trying to catch up on the sleep they had been missing due to the stress of recent events.

And in fact they saw nothing of their guests at all during the day. They just kept sleeping, going downstairs at odd times to bring up something to eat, until finally, when it was the following night, and everyone else had come back and gone to bed themselves, it did seem finally like they had made up for the sleep of which they had been deprived.

At around two a.m., in the pajamas he'd been wearing for nearly twenty-four hours, and lying in his bed looking up through the darkness, Benjamin thought he heard whispering downstairs, and since he was now feeling refreshed, got up quietly and went out into the hall and to the head of the stairs, where he got down on his knees, leaning forward and tilting his head slightly as he tried to make out the muffled conversation from below.

'Spying, Dad?'

Banging his head against the railing of the banister, Benjamin looked up to see Matt standing over him.

'What are you doing up, Matt?'

'Killer insomnia.'

The door at the other end of the hall was opened and Jason looked down at them from his room.

'Come spy with us,' Matt whispered.

'Let's take it into Matt's room,' Benjamin said, getting to his feet. He motioned for Jason to come down the hall, waited till they'd gone ahead of him, then followed them into the room and closed the door. 'As long as we're all awake,' he said, turning on the light, 'let's take stock.' He seated himself on the small chair by Matt's desk. 'Who wants to go first?'

Matt went over to get into his bed. 'First doing what?'

'Well, telling about your day, of course.'

'I will,' Jason said.

'Good, Jason. Go ahead.'

Jason began fluttering his hands beside his face, opened his eyes wide and began sticking his tongue in and out of his mouth.

149

'Those people are making us crazeee!'

'My turn?' Matt said.

'Thank you, Jason,' his father said as his son continued shaking his hands and making faces. 'Jason? Thank you?'

He stopped. 'You're welcome.'

'They're fraying our nerves to the breaking point,' Matt said.

'First of all,' Benjamin said, 'they're not "those people".'

'Dad, have mercy on us,' Matt said. 'We can't take any more.'

'And second of all,' Benjamin said, 'and above all else, they're our guests. And that carries a whole set of obligations. So let's think carefully about exactly what these obligations are, and what they mean, as we put them into practice. And see if we can't figure out why we have to treat a guest in our home differently, say, than someone we just happen to bump into on the street.'

'How come you were spying on them?' Jason said.

'I was concerned to see that they were sleeping comfortably and that all was well. But let's try again on our discussion. Now. From what little I've been able to tell, Aaron seems like a very nice kid.' Benjamin looked back and forth between his sons. 'Yes?'

'Yes what?' Matt said.

'Is he a nice kid?'

'I'm calling for a definition of "nice",' Jason said. 'Matt, where's your dictionary?'

Benjamin shook his head.

'I thought we should always agree on a definition of terms.'

'Not when we already know what it means.'

'Let me handle this,' Matt said, sitting up in his bed and raising his hand. It was quiet as they looked over at him. 'Dad, the kid's totally bonkers. Trust me.'

'Why is he bonkers?'

'It's genetic,' Jason said.

'No, I meant why as in what did he do that you're making this judgment about him?'

'Space people,' Matt said.

Benjamin nodded.

'Some are visible, some are invisible. Some are already here and some haven't got here yet.'

'We're expecting a shitload of them to land tomorrow,' Jason said.

'Okay,' Benjamin said, nodding, 'let's just —'

'You need to know how to greet them,' Matt said, placing the tips of his fingers together. 'Do this.'

'What I hear you saying is that he's an

imaginative kid.'

'Imaginative is when you know you're making it up,' Jason said.

'Dad,' Matt said, 'we don't want them to turn you inside out. Do what I'm showing you.'

Benjamin looked at them a few more moments.

'Do it.'

Benjamin placed the tips of his fingers together.

'Now say "Wago",' Matt said.

'Wago.'

'Now say it again.'

'Wago,' he said again.

'When you're approached by one,' Jason said, 'be sure and say it twice.'

'How do I know it's there,' Benjamin said, 'if it's an invisible one?'

'If it's an invisible one your hair will start waving back and forth.'

'Say it twice together,' Matt said. 'For your survival I need to be sure you're going to do it right.'

'Wago wago,' their father said.

'You're safe.'

'So, if the only way you know if you're being approached by an invisible one is that your hair starts waving,' Benjamin said, 'how does a bald person know he's being approached?'

The two of them looked at him for several moments. 'Dad,' Jason said finally, opening the door, 'you need some more sleep.'

Elaine was sitting up in bed and the lamp had been turned on beside her when Benjamin returned. 'What was that all about?' she said as he came into the room.

'Just chatting. Just unwinding with the boys.'

'What have they been doing all day?'

'Just enjoying their visitor,' he said, walking across the room.

'How have they been enjoying him?'

He stopped at the end of the bed. 'Just getting acquainted with him, Elaine.'

'You can't be more specific?'

Benjamin shrugged. 'Just learning new things from him.'

'Like?'

'Elaine.'

'You can't tell me what new things they're learning from him?'

'I don't know.' He shrugged again. 'I guess he knows some sort of space language.'

'Why am I not surprised?'

'Elaine,' he said, 'if you're going to be negative, why don't we just go back to sleep?'

'I'm going to be.'

153

He walked toward the bathroom. 'Then I'll brush my teeth and we'll go back to sleep.'

'How can I not be negative with those morons living under my roof?'

He stopped by the door.

'What would you call them?' she said.

'Well that's about the last thing.'

'How about phonies? Take your pick.'

He put his finger in his ear and wiggled it. 'My hearing must be going out.'

'You are so taken in by those people,' she said, getting down in the bed. 'It's pathetic.'

'Then tell me. What's phony about them?'

'That Garth?'

'Garth's a phony now?'

'Every inch.'

Benjamin shook his head. 'What are you talking about?'

'The other night? Sitting down there?'

'Right.'

'The man's a fraud.'

'Why?'

'Sitting over in the corner furrowing his brow while the rest of us were talking? Like he was having deep thoughts?'

'Elaine, he was having deep thoughts.'

'You are so conned, Benjamin,' she said. 'And Goya?'

'Let's hear what's wrong with Goya now.'

154

'Forget it.'

'An interesting and entertaining person,' Benjamin said, 'if you want my appraisal.'

'I'm sure it is.'

'Now let's hear yours.'

'Just forget it.' She got all the way down in the bed.

'Elaine, I have just finished giving the boys a lecture on how we treat guests in our home. I guess I should have included shitting on them behind their backs.'

'I can't take her, Benjamin.'

'Why not?'

Elaine pulled the covers up over her shoulder.

'Tell me.'

'The complete professional hippy,' Elaine said. 'I mean, Jesus, can't she give it a rest just once in a while?'

He looked down at her as she stared at the base of the lamp on the table. 'I really didn't know you felt like this. When we visited them — which you once said was something that changed our lives, and it did — you proclaimed we're all in this fight together, everyone doing it in their own way.'

'I've seen the light.'

'Well I hope at least you still think we're all dedicated to the same principles. As distasteful as you may find them personally.'

She shook her head. 'Not after the other night.'

'You won't even give them that?'

'Benjamin, what those people are dedicated to is driving around sponging off suckers like us. When they're not getting their big faces on as many TV news shows and in as many newspapers as they can find.'

'Publicity seekers you're calling them now?'

'In a word.'

'Jesus Christ, Elaine.'

'Don't Jesus Christ me, Benjamin. And their kids are a mess.'

'Oh, let's rip into their children now.'

'But that's what you have to look at, Benjamin.'

'And I do. And I find them expressive and involved.'

'Really?'

'In their own way, yes.'

'Tell me what that Nefertiti's involved in.'

'Life. To be a little trite.'

Elaine nodded. 'If life is sucking,' she said, 'then I'll agree with you.'

'Sucking?'

'And while I'm on the subject,' she said, looking up at him, 'do you think there's any chance you could keep your eyeballs in their sockets next time Goya is nursing her?'

He looked up at the ceiling. 'You're unbelievable.'

'No, I'm just not a triple-D. Benjamin, the point is you have some romantic notion in your head about these people — God knows where it came from — where they're the great shock troops of the movement, forging the way for the rest of us.'

'Of course that's what they are.'

'They're bums, Benjamin. Slobs. They're an embarrassment.' It was quiet for a long time, then she closed her eyes.

'Let's be a little harsh on our fellow man, shall we?' Benjamin said.

'Come back to bed.'

He walked into the bathroom. 'I had no idea you felt like this.'

'And one last thing,' she said from the other room. 'All I can say is, this had better work.'

He removed his toothbrush from the holder above the sink. Shaking his head, he squeezed a little toothpaste on it.

'Benjamin.'

'I'm brushing my teeth.' He turned on the faucet and held his brush under the water.

'Did you hear what I said?'

He put the brush into his mouth.

'Benjamin?'

157

He stepped back into the bedroom so he could see her.

'Did you hear what I said?' she repeated.

He nodded as he brushed.

'Because if it doesn't,' she said, 'the expression "all hell breaking loose" will have to be redefined.'

Benjamin held the brush still so he could answer. 'She'll be back home by the end of the week.'

'Benjamin, I can't take three more days.'

'And I'm sure you won't have to,' he said, reaching up to rub a drop of toothpaste off his lower lip. 'Probably she'll be gone tomorrow. But to be a hundred percent safe, I'm saying the end of the week.'

As it turned out, the prediction that the guest room would be vacated by the end of the week — let alone on the following day — was premature.

But Elaine's prophecy too, that a redefinition of 'all hell breaking loose' would result from the continuing presence of their guests, also remained unfulfilled. And in fact, as their residency in her home persisted, her reaction took a surprisingly different form, and she found herself staying in bed, sometimes watching TV, but more often, bored with the daytime programming, turning it off and going to sleep. Sometimes, when the others were out, she would go down to the kitchen to fix herself something to eat, but when she wasn't alone in the house she would send Benjamin down to bring up a bowl of cereal or a sandwich to eat in the bedroom.

Though annoyed, Benjamin was sensitive to the pressures his wife was experiencing with five extra bodies under her roof and, instead of demanding she be more attentive to their guests, he placated her as best he could with assurances of their impending departure. On one occasion he brought a small package of pills back from the drugstore which the pharmacist had told him would boost Elaine's energy level. But instead of taking one she muttered something under her breath about an enema, which Benjamin couldn't hear and she wouldn't repeat, then put the pills on the bedside table and turned over to go back to sleep.

It was in the supermarket one afternoon that the reason for Benjamin's miscalculation about the swift departure of his mother-in-law became evident to him. He was there with Goya and her children, shopping for dinner. Aaron and Nefertiti had gone off on their own.

'What's with these naps of Elaine's?' Goya said as they turned into the produce aisle. She grabbed a bunch of carrots from a shelf to drop in the cart Benjamin was pushing. 'Has she always done that?'

'It's a new feature.'

'It kind of casts a pall,' Goya said, 'if you don't mind my saying so.'

'It's all tied up with her mother being here,' Benjamin said.

'Those two,' Goya said. 'A cat and a dog.'

'There's a little friction there,' Benjamin said.

Goya removed a head of lettuce from the next shelf. She studied it a moment, then held it in front of Benjamin.

'What?'

'Look at it.'

'I am.'

She pointed to a dried white drop on one of its leaves. 'I mean, why don't they just spray the people down here,' she said, tossing it back onto the shelf. 'Cut out the middle man.'

'Actually we belong to an organic food co-op, but their delivery truck always seems to break down on our day.'

Goya pushed the cart on a little farther. 'Get that wife and mother-in-law of yours talking to each other,' she said. 'Get them in a Circle together, that's what somebody should do.'

'A circle?' Benjamin said.

'Maybe I'll put them in one,' she said. 'In fact, I'm going to make a point of it.'

'What's a circle?'

'What is one?'

'In the sense you're using it.'

'A Circle of Agamemnon.'

'Oh, okay.'

Suddenly Aaron and Nefertiti ran around the end of the aisle, Nefertiti holding up a jar as they hurried up to them.

'What's that?' Goya said.

'Wheat germ,' Aaron said.

She shook her head. 'You'll spoil your dinner.'

'But we'll save it till later.'

'Oh no,' Goya said. 'I know you.'

'Please!' Nefertiti said, holding it up in front of her mother's face. 'Please! It's toasted!'

'Put it back, Neffi.' She pointed down the aisle. 'Now.'

The children turned around and walked slowly away.

'Kids are a kick in the head, aren't they?' Goya said.

'They are,' Benjamin said. 'But listen, I don't think you should put Elaine and her mother in a Circle of Agamemnon.'

'Why not?'

'Unless it's a very big one.'

'Did you notice the dress Neffi's wearing today?'

'I did,' Benjamin said. 'Interesting material.'

'It's calico.'

'Oh?'

'The real shit,' Goya said as they moved along past the celery. 'There's only a couple places in the country you can get it. We went four hundred miles out of our way last time we were driving across, to a little store down in Missouri.'

'Really?'

She stepped to the other side of the aisle and picked up a small bunch of bananas, squinting at its label. 'Honduras,' she said, tossing it back. 'How many dead peasants do you suppose it took to grow those?' She returned across the aisle. 'I mean, we could have ordered it,' she said as they continued along the aisle with their cart.

'Ordered what?'

'The calico. But it was a good excuse to show the kids more of the country. They'd never seen a redneck before.'

'Historical,' Benjamin said. 'Calico. The old west.'

'I really should make Neffi wash it out one of these days,' Goya said, holding a squash in front of Benjamin.

'What's wrong with that?'

'You don't want to know.' She put it back. 'Garth made that dress for Neffi, by the way. Needle and thread. Next time she comes back I'll show you the seams. Straight as a fucking pencil.'

'No sewing machine?' Benjamin said.

'Say sewing machine in front of Garth and he'll go apoplectic.'

Benjamin shook his head. 'What an amazing guy.' He watched as she removed an apple from one of the bins to hold up against her ear.

'God, that fire out in LA,' she said as she put it back. 'Scary.'

'Was there a big one?'

'No I mean the house.'

'What house?'

'Behind your mother-in-law's.'

They walked to the end of the aisle.

'Elaine told you about that?'

'Elaine? God no. Sleeping Beauty hasn't said two words to us since we got here. Listen, Ben, you four really need to drag your butts up to Vermont to live if you want Elaine to come to life again. Deathchester County, that's what this place is.'

163

'So you didn't hear about the fire from Elaine,' Benjamin said.

'I didn't hear about it myself, actually.'

'Who heard about it?'

'Garth.'

'Oh, okay.'

'He passed it along.'

Benjamin nodded.

'So what have we got here now?' Goya reached down into the cart and began sorting through the products they had selected. She removed one of the boxes to look at. 'Do you trust oats in a box?' she said.

'I tend to.'

'You do trust oats in a box . . .'

'I have to say I do. They've never done anything to betray my trust.'

She put them back in the cart.

'So Garth's the one who heard about the fire, then?' Benjamin said.

'I haven't really gotten to know her yet,' Goya said.

'Who?'

'Elaine's mother.'

Goya took a package from the cart with a picture on it of a smiling boy with smudges of chocolate all over his cheeks and chin as he opened his mouth wide to take a bite from a large, horseshoe-shaped piece of chocolate candy. 'I'm just getting this for a souvenir.'

'So Garth and Elaine's mother have been speaking then?' Benjamin said.

'Well, he fixed that toilet for her.'

'Oh?'

'Put Garth in front of a broken toilet and he's a pig in shit.'

'I didn't know Garth fixed that for her.'

'The second night we were here,' she said, returning the package of candy. 'And the rest, as they say, is history. Let's get the hell out of here.' She pushed the cart on ahead of him toward the checkout stands.

Benjamin stayed behind a few moments, looking down at the floor of the super-market, then caught up with her. 'What do you mean?' he said.

'About what?'

'The rest, as they say, is history.'

She pushed the cart to the end of one of the lines leading to a checkout stand and reached down for a box of raisins. 'We made these ourselves one year. Grew the grapes and everything. Put them all out on trays in the back. Of course by the time they were dried every fruit fly in New England was calling our place home.' She dropped them back in the cart.

'Goya?'

'What?'

'The rest, as they say, is history.'

'What about it?'

'I didn't quite understand the reference.'

'The man has an appetite,' she said. 'What can I tell you?' She shrugged. 'I made peace with that years ago.'

'An appetite?'

'Just wash it off before you bring it home,' she said. 'Other than that, do what you want.'

Again Benjamin looked down at the floor as Goya moved a space forward in line. 'Wash it off before you bring it home?' he said.

'That's all I ask of him,' she said. 'Benjamin, I made peace with this years ago. I'm married to a goddamn genius, for Christ's sake. Cut him some slack, right? If that's his thing.'

Benjamin nodded.

'What do I need a pissed-off genius on my hands for?' She looked around at the other people in the store. 'Hey, Benjamin, all these suburban types packed in here like sardines. God, maybe this is some kind of giant trap and it's slowly closing in on us and it's going to crush us all together and we're all going to wind up in a tin with a key on it. Here come those nutty kids again.' She opened her arms and Aaron and Nefertiti ran into them. She held them tightly against herself for several seconds, then looked down at one of Nefertiti's hands behind her back. 'What have you got?'

Nefertiti stepped back, keeping her hand behind her.

'Come on,' Goya said, 'I saw it.'

Nefertiti shook her head.

'Come on, Neffi.' She reached behind her daughter to grab her hand, then removed a small package from it. She laughed. 'Look at this,' she said, holding it in front of Benjamin.

He nodded. 'Yeast,' he said.

She turned back to the girl. 'What do you want yeast for?'

'I just want it.'

Laughing, she dropped it in the cart. 'Are kids a kick in the head or what?' she said.

'Totally,' Benjamin said.

Still laughing, she pushed her cart another space forward. 'Are your kids this crazy?'

But Benjamin didn't answer. His eyes had fallen to the cover of a tabloid at the end of the checkout stand from which the green and grinning face of a Martian stared back at him.

Elaine carried the two cups of coffee down the stairs and to the closed door of her mother's room. She pushed at the door with her elbow, but when it didn't open she set one of the cups on the floor long enough to turn the knob and open it.

For a moment or two she looked at the sleeping form of her mother, turned toward the wall with the blankets pulled up over most of her head. Then she went to the small table beside the bed and set one of the cups down on her book. She carried the other one across the room, lowered the seat of the toilet, then sat down, lifting the cup of hot coffee to her mouth to blow across its surface.

Finally she cleared her throat, softly, but there was no movement from under the blankets.

Elaine took a small sip of coffee, again clearing her throat, more loudly.

After a moment the blankets moved slightly.

She watched as her mother lifted her head a few inches up from the pillow.

'Good morning,' she said again.

After another pause, her mother twisted her face around to look at her.

'Elaine?'

'I brought you a cup of coffee. It's there on the table.'

Her mother looked at it.

'Sugar, no milk.'

Her mother reached up to push some hair from her face, then after another moment or two turned all the way over in the bed toward her daughter.

'It's hot, so be careful.'

'Well darling,' her mother said, looking at her wristwatch, 'that's very thoughtful. But it's a little early for me.'

Elaine took another small sip from her coffee.

'I'd like to get another hour or two of sleep.'

'I wanted to talk.'

'Well yes,' her mother said, 'but could it wait till later?'

'It's kind of urgent.'

Her mother looked back at the cup of coffee on her book, then raised herself up enough to remove the pillow from under her head and rest it against the wall behind her. 'Is there some problem?' she said, moving herself up to lean against the pillow.

'Not really. But I just think it's time to move along now.'

Again her mother glanced at her watch. 'Darling, it's the middle of the night for me.' She reached over for her coffee.

'That's hot.'

'You said that.' She raised the cup to her

lips, taking a small sip. 'Move along. What does that mean, dear?'

'It means we've all had a great visit. It's been wonderful seeing you again. The boys have loved it.' She nodded.

'And it's time to go?'

'Yes.'

The two women looked at each other in silence for a moment.

'Well, has something happened?'

'No. But we've managed to be relatively civil to each other up until now and I want us both to make the effort to end things on that note.' She glanced over at the large statue of a headless horseman in the corner.

'That goes on top of my television when I get back so I'll think of my two little angels every time I turn it on.'

'So tell me what airline you came on and I'll go make a reservation for later today.'

'But dear, what's upset you?'

'I'm not upset,' Elaine said, getting up from the toilet, 'but I think the most important thing is ending the visit on a high note. What airline?'

After a few more moments, Nan moved to the edge of her bed and reached across the space between them to take her daughter's hand. 'Dear, look at me.' She gave her hand a squeeze. 'Look at me.'

'Mother, I am looking directly at you and have been since I came down here.'

'Now tell me how I can help if you won't say what's on your mind?'

'Oh God, I hoped it could end on a high note,' Elaine said, looking up at the ceiling.

'What could end — my visit?'

'Your visit.'

'But it's not ending.'

'Wrong.' She pulled her hand out of her mother's and went to the doorway. 'I'll call Pan Am.'

'I came on United.'

'A return ticket?'

'Yes.'

'I'll book your seat.'

'Elaine,' her mother said before she could leave, 'we'll talk about a seat after you've told me what's bothering you. Not before.'

Elaine looked down at a pair of pink fuzzy slippers beside the bed.

'I'm quite serious,' her mother said.

For a long time it was quiet. 'When Dad left me this house,' she said finally, 'even though there was no specific reference in his will, no particular codicil or whatever you call it, but I sort of think — this is just a guess, but knowing his feelings about things as well as I do I think it's probably a fairly good one — I sort of don't think it

'Garth's such a gentle soul. That would devastate him.'

'I'm sure Benjamin will be more tactful than I was,' she said, going the rest of the way up the stairs and taking the handle of the kitchen door.

'Are you going to call the airline now?'

'I am.'

'Well may I make my own reservation?'

'I'll be happy to.'

'Well I know you would,' her mother said, coming up the stairs after her, 'but you've all pampered me so much already, I need to feel I can still do something for myself.'

Elaine held the door as her mother went past her into the kitchen.

'I'll need to call Information first for the number.'

'Fine,' Elaine said, following her.

They stood quietly a few moments.

Elaine glanced at the phone on the wall, then back at her mother.

'I know where the phone is, dear.'

'Information is four-one-one.'

'May I say one very small little thing first?'

Elaine reached over to remove the phone's receiver. 'Make the reservation,' she said, holding it out to her, 'then you can say one very small little thing while you're packing.'

'About Garth.'

'Mother.'

'Because I have learned so so very much from him, Elaine. About what you and Benjamin are accomplishing. You know, I had absolutely no idea of the larger importance of what the two of you are doing with the boys.'

'It's not going to work.' She stepped toward the wall.

'Dear.'

'I will call,' Elaine said.

'I said I'd do it.'

'Then do it.'

'I just thought you'd want to know about the excitement Garth has conveyed to me about what you all are doing,' she said, taking the receiver.

'Call.'

'You know, Elaine,' she said, turning to the phone. 'You can be very cruel.'

'I wonder where I got that from?'

Her mother dialled a number, waited a moment, then dialled another.

'There's one more,' Elaine said when she paused again.

'One more what?'

'Number.'

'Dear, would you agree that there are some unresolved issues between us?'

'Just one.' Elaine reached toward the

telephone. 'You're still here.'

Nan moved her daughter's hand away from the dial.

'Mother,' Elaine said, 'may I say something you might not like to hear?'

'I'm waiting for you to say something I'd like to hear.'

'May I tell you something I've never told you before?'

'Be my guest.'

'It's that I changed when I got away from you, and everybody who knew me before said, "My God, you're not the same person you used to be. You used to be this vain little nothing with beautifully brushed hair. And now you talk and laugh and think of interesting and clever things to say." When I got away from you, Mother, I became a person. For the first time in my life.'

'You were always a person, Elaine.'

'No!'

'But they're right about your hair,' she said, hanging up the phone. 'I haven't wanted to say anything, but you really should give it more attention.'

'Look what I've turned into since you've come!'

'Ten minutes brushing a day, that's all it needs.'

Her mother replaced the receiver, but

176

Elaine removed it again.

'Ignoring people when I go out shopping? Snubbing them? Putting on Benjamin's dark glasses before I go out now — if I ever do — so no one will come up to me? I'm a friendly person, Mother. Or was. Or became one. But not any more. I've become the horrible snobby little person again that you trained me to be.'

'These are hurtful words, darling.'

Her mother placed her hand on the receiver but Elaine pulled it away.

'My children? Who are they? I don't even know them any more. I can't even think of anything to say to my own children any more. Since you got here, all I can do is escape into sleep.'

'Dear, none of that's my fault.'

'Then whose?'

'I have no idea. Maybe you're starting your change of life a little early.'

Elaine began dialling, but her mother pulled her hand away from the phone. 'Is that a possibility, dear?'

'That I'm menopausal?'

'I'm just casting around.'

'My only hot flash is you, Mother.' Again she tried to dial and again her mother pulled her hand away.

'Stop it, Mother.'

'You stop it.'

Elaine began to dial another time, batting her mother's hand away when she tried to stop her.

'This is so childish, dear.'

'Yes, because I have reverted to a child state!'

'Then you need to revert back.'

'Which I plan to do. As soon as you're over Kansas.'

Nan reached for the receiver but her daughter pulled her hand away. 'I'm not sure we go over Kansas.'

'New Jersey then. Why waste time?'

'For one thing, darling, I can't leave here with it in your mind that somehow I'm responsible for these problems you're having.' She grabbed the receiver but her daughter tightened her grip on it. 'And I really didn't force myself on you, you know. Ben did invite me, if you'll recall.'

'Not to spend the rest of your goddamn life with us!' She yanked on it but her mother yanked back.

'Well I know it was just to fuck the principal and toddle off again.'

'And thank you for that, Mother. Maybe I haven't thanked you enough for that yet. Maybe you're waiting for me to express more fully the deep debt of gratitude I feel that you fucked Principal Claymore for us.'

Nan shrugged. 'It was nothing.'

'So now you've been thanked! Leave us alone!!' Elaine began prying her mother's fingers away from the instrument but Nan quickly put her other hand around it and yanked at it again.

'What about your neighbors, Mother, shouldn't you be getting back to them? The Van Nordhoffs? Maybe in his great grief over losing his home you can think of some interesting way of providing comfort to Mr Van Nordhoff.' Continuing to twist the receiver in her mother's hand, Elaine pulled it slowly back toward her.

'Van Noordstrom, dear.'

'Him too.'

Although Nan put her other hand around the receiver, Elaine kept twisting and tugging it slowly back with both of hers till finally it broke free. Gripping it tightly, Elaine banged against the stove, and then fell down on a knee to the floor. Part of the long cord had become wrapped around her mother as they had struggled and she began pulling it away from her chest, then they looked over to see Goya and her daughter walk into the room and to the sink.

Goya turned on the water. 'Can you reach?'

Nefertiti stretched her hands up and began rubbing them together under the water.

'Very clean, Neffi,' Goya said.

'I am.'

'Extra clean,' Goya said, 'because when you're finished I'm going to let you do something for the very first time.'

'What's that?'

'I'm going to let you put two people into a Circle of Agamemnon all by yourself.'

Jason's expression of interest in medieval armor had come, coincidentally, just when Benjamin had seen a review in the *New York Times* on a book on that very subject. It wasn't on the library's order list, and since the only establishment in Hastings remotely resembling a bookstore was a side-street boutique selling tracts from Indian swamis along with its beads and small colored glass balls, it was necessary for someone to make a quick trip into the city for it. And this was the reason — accurate as far as it went — given by Benjamin to Garth for joining him on his morning commute, though clearly the more urgent purpose was to find a polite but forcible way of telling him the time had arrived for a separation of the two families.

Even though most seats were already filled

by commuters who had boarded at previous stops, they managed to find two seats side by side, and for several minutes after they left the station Garth sat quietly next to Benjamin, pressing his fingers against his eyes.

'You okay?' Benjamin said finally.

Garth nodded, keeping his fingers in place.

'Tired, I guess,' Benjamin said.

'Beat to holy shit.'

They rode awhile without talking.

'I guess Goya clued you in about the basement scene,' Garth said finally.

'She did.'

'She thinks I should have asked your permission.'

'For what?'

Garth shook his head. 'Goya can get like that — something sticks in her head and she won't quit, I swear to God. "They're our hosts, Garth, you don't start banging people's relatives in their home without asking." '

'Oh no.'

'I probably should have, man.'

'No permission needed.'

'In my defense,' Garth said, 'your mother-in-law did make the first move.'

'No problem. Really.'

181

They rode quietly for a few moments. Benjamin was about to speak again when Garth said, 'I'm down there, you know, fixing her crapper, and all of a sudden she starts in on me about . . .' He made his hands into fists and began turning them in his eyes. 'But you don't want the gory details.'

Benjamin shrugged. 'If it helps to get them off your chest.'

'Okay, well I get the goddamn shitter working for her and stand up again and there she is over on the bed, tears streaming down.'

'Tears streaming down.'

'Bawling like a faucet.'

'Really.'

'It was fucking pitiful.'

Benjamin looked past Garth and out the window at the Hudson River.

'So I'm taken aback, you know. "You okay?" I say. "Garth, I haven't been okay for a long time," she says. And she starts in about the dead husband. Feeling his presence in the house. Some dream she had the other night about seeing him standing there beside the bed. By the way, she'd kept herself pure for the guy over the years. No pussy for nobody. You might not have known that.'

'No.'

'Well she wouldn't mention it,' Garth said, 'you being family and all. But staying true to his memory, all that shit, it's been a big deal for her. And I guess she gets hit on a lot. She's older, but . . .' He pulled his fists away from his face and opened his eyes very wide a couple of times.

'But what?' Benjamin said.

'What?'

'She's older but what, you were going to say?'

Garth frowned at the back of the seat ahead of them for a moment, then shook his head. 'Can't remember what the fuck I was going to say.'

'Garth,' Benjamin said, 'listen, there's no problem with that — permission not needed — but there is one thing . . .'

'Will you be my husband tonight?' Garth said.

'I'm sorry?'

'I finish drying off my hands, you know. On and on she's still going about resisting temptation and all this. Then out she comes with that.'

'Will you be my husband tonight?'

'What the fuck could I say, man?'

'You had no choice.'

'I didn't feel I did.'

183

'You've made a lonely woman happy,' Benjamin said.

'Well that's how I look at it,' Garth said. 'I mean, I'll be honest with you, I've never been one to pass up a good fuck.' He glanced at the seat ahead of them again. 'Or a bad one either, come to think of it.' He looked back at Benjamin. 'But Jesus Christ, man, let me give you a friendly piece of advice.'

'What's that?'

'Next time an older broad comes on to you, I would very strongly suggest you think of some subtle way of finding out how long it's been since she's had a dick in her.'

Benjamin nodded. 'I'll try to remember that.'

'And if it's been over five years . . .'

'Garth listen,' Benjamin said as they slowed for the next station, 'I don't mean to change the subject —'

'So fine,' he said. 'Husband-for-a-night. I can live with that. I'm a groggy piece of shit the next day, but if that's the price of bringing a little sunshine into someone's life . . .'

'Garth.'

'Fast-forward to night two. So there I am, sleeping away on your living-room floor — one a.m., two, whatever — and I feel this hand jiggling my shoulder. I open my eyes.

184

'Garth?' she's whispering to me. 'I'm still getting a little drip down there. Can you come look at it?'

'Here's the thing,' Benjamin said as the train stopped and the doors slid open for the next batch of commuters, 'first of all, you and I haven't talked about the whole home-education thing, which we really need to do.'

'Got to.'

'But Garth,' Benjamin said, 'and I really don't want you to take this the wrong way . . .'

'Hey buddy.' Garth put his hand on Benjamin's knee. 'Don't you take this the wrong way either. I love your family. We all do. You guys knock us out. But I didn't see this freight train coming — not the one we're on, the one back there — so we're going to be checking out a little earlier than planned.' He patted Benjamin's knee.

'You're leaving?'

'Hey, don't take it that way. You guys are the best. I mean that. The greatest ever. But man. What can I tell you?' He shook his head, blinking. 'But we'll be back before you know it.'

'I hope so.'

'Count on it. And that little cabin of ours up in Vermont? We'll put your and Elaine's name on the door whenever you want.'

Benjamin nodded. 'We may take you up on that.'

'But not just the cabin,' Garth said. 'Anything that comes up. Whatever happened with that asshole principal that was trying to fuck you guys over?'

'I guess you could say he backed off.'

'You faced the bastard down.'

'In a way.'

'Good man.' He patted Benjamin's knee again. 'But if the son of a bitch starts up just let me know . . . I'll get on the evening news down here and scare him shitless.'

'I think he's under control.'

'But you'll let me know if he kicks up?'

Benjamin nodded.

'I mean it.'

'Definitely.'

'Good buddy,' Garth said, 'I'm an ear to listen and a hand to help. Don't you forget that.'

They rode quietly for a few moments, then Benjamin looked down at Garth's hand as it slid slowly off his knee. Garth's chin fell down against his chest, where it remained, Garth snoring softly, till the train had pulled into Grand Central Station.

■ ■ ■ ■

# THREE

■ ■ ■ ■

Holding the bag from Brentano's, Benjamin opened the front door of his house. In the chair across the room, legs stretched out in front of her, his mother-in-law sat with her head tilted back, her face covered with a damp washcloth.

Benjamin stepped inside and closed the door.

Nefertiti was lying on the sofa, her head resting in her mother's lap. Goya's shirt had been pulled up and she slowly caressed her daughter's hair as she sucked on a breast, glancing up at Benjamin, but then looking back down at her nursing daughter.

'Is Elaine around?' Benjamin said.

Looking back up quickly, Goya put her finger to her lips.

'Oh sorry.' Benjamin nodded. 'Sorry.'

Goya continued stroking the girl's hair.

'Elaine around?' Benjamin whispered.

Goya glanced at the stairway.

189

As he walked past Nan's chair, Benjamin's shoe knocked over a drinking glass on the floor, spilling some brown fluid and a tiny leaf-covered twig that had been in the glass. He bent down to pick up the twig, studying it for a moment, then holding it out to Goya. 'What's this?' he whispered.

She shook her head without looking up.

Elaine was standing in the center of the bedroom. 'What's that all about?' Benjamin said as he came into the room. He closed the door behind him. 'Downstairs. What in hell's that all about?'

'Did you?' she said.

'Did I what?'

'Tell him to leave.'

'Garth? Of course.'

'And are they?'

'Of course.'

'When?'

'Later today, I believe.'

'You believe.'

'Later today.'

'Mother's not,' Elaine said.

'She's not?'

She stared silently at him.

'Nan's not leaving?'

'No.'

'Well did you talk to her?'

'Yes.'

190

'And did you use the whorehouse line?'

'Whorehouse,' she said. 'Brothel.'

'Brothel.'

'Benjamin.'

'Did you say whorehouse or brothel?'

'It wouldn't have mattered.'

'We discussed this,' he said, setting the book down on the bed. 'We agreed brothel wasn't strong enough.'

'Benjamin.'

'It sounds like you pulled your big punch.'

'It would not the fuck have mattered if I had said whorehouse or brothel,' she said loudly.

'Okay. Okay.' He held up his hands.

'So what are you going to do now?' she said.

'Me?'

'Yes, you.'

He lowered his hands. 'Okay. Well. I'm going to go down and tell her to leave.'

'Then do it.'

'All right,' he said. 'I'm going to.'

'Now.'

'Elaine, if I had some small inkling of what in hell has been going on here in my absence I could more effectively impart that instruction.'

'Now!'

Except for Nefertiti having been moved to

the other breast, nothing had changed in the living room. None of the three females looked up as Benjamin reached the foot of the stairs. Beside him Nan remained stretched out in the chair, her face still covered with the pink cloth. Benjamin seated himself on the bottom stair.

'Benjamin!' Goya whispered from across the room.

He looked up to see her motioning for him to come.

'I need to have a word with my mother-in-law.'

She continued to motion to him. 'We need to talk.'

'In a minute.'

'Something happened while you were gone,' she said.

He looked back at her a few moments, then got up and went across the room.

Goya moved herself and her daughter a little farther over on the sofa. 'Sit down.'

'I'd just as soon stand.'

'Something happened while you were gone that you need to know about.' She began patting on the cushion beside her.

He looked down at it. 'Just for a second then,' he said, wedging himself in tightly between Goya and the end of the sofa.

'What happened?'

The top of the child's head rubbed against his elbow as she suckled.

'Did Garth tell you we were leaving?'

'He did.'

'Because we can't now.'

Nefertiti burped.

'Why not?'

Suddenly Goya's breast came out of Nefertiti's mouth, spraying a small stream of milk around until the girl could put her lips back around it.

'Why can't you?'

'Nan needs me here.' She held out a piece of cloth to Benjamin.

'Why does she need you here?'

'To help her back out of the Circle.'

Benjamin shook his head. 'No. Look, Goya . . .'

As she reached across her daughter to rub at a wet spot on the fly of Benjamin's pants, he glanced up to see Elaine, halfway down the stairs, turning around and starting back up.

'Excuse me.'

She was standing at the far end of the hallway. 'Here's the plan,' she said as he approached her.

'Elaine, if you'd just told me what kind of crazy shit has been going on here while —'

She put her forefinger on his lips. 'You

193

can't hear the plan if you're talking.'

'The plan is that you tell me what happened and I go back down and clear them out.'

She reached up to a short rope coming down from the ceiling. 'What happened,' she said, pulling down on the rope and lowering a narrow wooden stairway, 'was that Mother and I had a brawl, and Goya came in on her side.'

Benjamin looked up into the dark opening at the top of the stairway.

'Now you know what happened. Go clear them out.' She started up the stairs.

'Well don't go up there.'

'When everyone but immediate family members are out of this house,' she said, continuing to climb, 'I shall descend. Not before.' She reached the top and stepped onto a wooden platform, then bent down to begin pulling the stairway up after her.

'Wait a minute, Elaine.' He took hold of the stairs to stop them from rising farther. 'Wait a minute.'

'I'm sorry I interrupted you and Goya down there. You were having such fun. But why don't you go in and get Matt's GI Joe Super Shot squirt gun this time so she won't have the advantage.'

194

'They're not leaving after all,' Benjamin said.

'They're not.'

'No. Which means one thing — there's never been a time like this for the four of us to stick together.'

'Let go of the stairs.'

'We need an emergency family meeting, Elaine, to start reclaiming our turf. As a unit. Acting together. That's what's been missing up till now. Where are the boys?'

'At the town pool.'

'The town pool's closed now.'

'Yes, but if you're standing in an empty swimming pool when aliens land they'll appoint you as rulers over your fellow humans.'

'Come on. We'll go find them.'

'Matt wants to be King of Tarrytown.'

Benjamin pulled the stairway the rest of the way down again.

'Unless you want that job.'

He started up the steps.

'Please don't come up here.'

'We'll use this as our base of operations,' he said as he reached the top.

'It's my base of operations.'

'Our command post.' He stepped onto the platform in the dark attic, then waved his hand through the air till it hit a string hang-

195

ing from above.

'Go back down, Benjamin. Try again to make them leave. As you promised.'

'That was the old plan.' He pulled the string and dim light filled the attic. 'The new one is that we generate a strategy between the four of us and treat this as a project. In survival. Social survival. How does a social unit — our family in this case — in the face of an external threat, come together and formulate a method of self-protection?'

Suddenly Elaine's mouth opened and she jumped back, raising one of her arms to point past Benjamin.

'What?' he said, turning around.

There were wooden beams running out from the platform to the far end of the attic, with thick pads of insulation between them. On one of the pads, turned upside down, was a large wooden trap, coming out from under it the hindquarters of a rat and its long hairless tail.

'Take it easy,' Benjamin said.

'Get it out.'

He nodded. 'I will. But the four of us have finally been pushed all the way, Elaine. Our backs are to the wall and we have no choice but to . . .'

'Get it out!'

Keeping his feet on the tops of two beams he slowly walked to the overturned trap and carefully picked it up. Pinned by its neck to the wood by the strong spring, the body of the rat hung down from the trap as he slowly lifted it up from the insulation pad.

'Is it dead?'

'Very dead, Elaine.'

'Get it out.'

'I think you said that.'

She stepped back to the far edge of the platform and watched as he slowly came back across the beams, the heavy body of the rat swaying slightly as he held it out to his side.

'Are you sure it's dead?'

'Do you understand what I'm saying about the four of us having been inexorably, inch by inch, forced into this wholly untenable —'

'Answer me!'

'It's either dead, Elaine, or a very sound sleeper.' He stepped back onto the platform. 'But may we please keep our priorities straight here?'

'The priority is to get it the fuck out!'

'No,' he said, 'it's to — '

*'Goddamn you, Benjamin.'*

'Right.'

He carried it down the stairs and, as soon

197

as he had reached the hallway, turned to see the steps rising back up and into the ceiling. Then there was a sharp metallic click.

He stood looking up at the large rectangular panel in the ceiling above his head. Then he reached up and took hold of the short length of rope dangling from it. He pulled.

'Elaine?'

He pulled on it again, harder.

'We don't lock doors, Elaine.'

There was no sound from above.

Finally he let go of it and turned toward the other end of the hall. He could hear the voices of Goya and her daughter coming from the living room.

'Eight times six,' Goya said.

'Forty-eight.'

'Nine times three.'

'Twenty-seven,' Nefertiti said.

He looked at the body hanging down from the trap in his hand and at one of the rat's tiny clawed feet. He looked at the piece of cheese, still clenched between its jaws. Then he walked to the end of the hallway and slowly down to the living room again, holding the trap slightly behind himself as he stopped beside his mother-in-law's chair.

Goya and her daughter were on the sofa where they had been before.

'Twelve times five,' Goya said.

The girl turned her head so her mother's breast came out of her mouth. 'Fifty-five.'

'Again.'

'It's not fifty-five?'

'That's five times eleven.'

'Okay let me think.'

'What's behind you?' Goya said, looking across the room at Benjamin.

'What?'

'What are you holding behind you?'

Benjamin moved his hip against the side of Nan's chair, pushing it an inch or so along the floor. Nan tilted her head forward and reached up to lift a corner of the damp cloth. 'Oh Jesus Christ!! Shit!!' She lurched backwards, twisting her head away and slamming the back of the chair into the wall as the cloth flew off her face.

'Just ridding the house of an unwanted visitor,' Benjamin said, carrying the dead rodent past her and to the kitchen.

But the rat was the only visitor he was able to eject.


A number of years before, events had occurred in the lives of Benjamin, Elaine and Nan which were momentous, and they had altered not only the course of those three individuals' lives, but the course of the lives of those around them. During the early years of their marriage the young couple had discussed and analyzed these events ad infinitum, sometimes with much emotion; but gradually, as their growing children demanded their attention, the subject came up less and less frequently, until finally they both decided there was no purpose in rehashing it further, and agreed to leave it behind.

But with Nan the subject had never been broached. Once or twice Benjamin had suggested to his wife that they might engage her mother in a discussion of those events as a way of trying to clear the air (there was a tension in their relationship with her that exceeded the usual strains occurring between married children and a parent), but he was always quick to realize the truth of Elaine's observation that such a discussion would only be viewed by Nan as a reopening of old wounds, and predictably her reaction would be an eruption of the hysteria that had characterized her behavior when the events were fresh.

Obviously the question of whether or not to discuss these matters with Goya had never arisen, since she was unaware of them, or at least unaware of them until she decided to go upstairs as Benjamin, in the kitchen, was busy wrapping the rat in numerous plastic bags that had come back from the supermarket.

Goya looked into their bedroom first, walking far enough inside to see in the bathroom. 'Elaine? Are you in there?' After another moment she went back into the hallway and opened the door to Matt's room, looking in to see that it was empty. She walked down the hall and looked in Jason's room, then came back to the middle of the hallway. 'Are you up here somewhere, Elaine?' She stood quietly waiting for an answer, and when there was none, called again. 'Elaine?'

Finally there was a click over her head and the stairs were partially lowered.

Goya took a step back to look up into the attic.

'What do you want, Goya?'

'Why are you up there?'

'Did you want something?'

'Just to talk. If that's not a problem.'

After another few seconds, Goya took hold of the bottom step and pulled the stairs all the way down.

Elaine watched her climb up toward her.

'Benjamin just about sent Nan into a convulsion dangling a dead rat in her face,' Goya said, stepping onto the platform beside her and looking around the dimly lit room.

'Goya, may I say something? Not that it's a big deal, but you know Nan is sort of the name the boys have for their grandmother. Benjamin and I use it too, so that we all —'

'She asked us to call her that.'

It was quiet for a moment.

Elaine nodded. 'Of course,' she said. 'Sorry.'

'Elaine, why do you always have to be so fucking defensive with me?'

'Goya,' she said, 'I think it's time for you and your family to start thinking of going home.'

Goya looked up at one of the slanting beams of the ceiling. 'I'm sure you do.'

'I do.'

'And what happens to Nan after we go?' Goya said.

'What happens to her?'

'We can't leave her in this poisonous atmosphere.'

'Then take her with you.'

The platform on which they were standing was made of rough wooden boards, and there was a small pile of newspapers resting on one corner of it. Goya removed a newspaper from just under the top one and opened it to spread over part of the platform.

'Goya.'

She flattened the newspaper down and then seated herself cross-legged on it. 'Things can't go on this way, Elaine.'

Elaine looked down at her. 'Goya, forgive me for sounding like a property-owning asshole, but this is not your house.'

'The earth is my house.'

'The earth maybe. But not this particular thing sitting on it.'

Goya shook her head. 'I'm sad for you, Elaine.'

'I'm sad that you're sad.'

There was a short piece of wire next to where Goya was sitting. She picked it up and bent it between her fingers. 'By the way,' she said, unbending it again, 'I know what happened back then.'

Elaine looked down at her without answering.

'With the three of you,' Goya said.

Elaine watched her form the wire into a circle.

'She told you about that?'

'She told Garth.'

Elaine nodded. 'Right. Well it happened. It was a long time ago.'

'But Elaine,' Goya said, looking up at her,

203

'Did you?'

'I like to think I always try a little love.'

'Not since we've been here you haven't.'

It was quiet for a few moments, then Elaine nodded. 'You're right, Goya. About that you are right. A little love I haven't tried yet.' She lowered herself down onto the newspaper, seating herself cross-legged in front of Goya. 'Now. What exactly did she tell Garth?'

Goya shrugged. 'Just that you were marrying this doctor — med student, whatever — and Benjamin broke into the church and kidnapped you.'

'And dragged me off to a cult.'

'And even though Nan wouldn't say this to your face — she is sensitive to your feelings, whether you like to think so or not — but since she's been here she's begun noticing that some of the brainwashing's seeped back in.'

'The brainwashing's seeped back in.'

'In little ways.'

'Such as?'

'A glazed expression.'

'Really.'

'That's the main one.'

'Do you think I have a glazed expression, Goya?'

'I didn't know you back then. I have no

means of comparison. And I realize you underwent extensive deprogramming . . .'

Elaine held up her hand. 'May I please give you the reality-based version now, Goya?'

Goya's hair was falling down across her shoulders. She tipped her head back and shook it slightly so the hair fell down over her back.

'My parents pushed me into the wedding with Carl to keep me away from Benjamin. Carl had proposed, but I hadn't made up my mind yet. They made it up for me.'

'So what's Carl doing today?'

'Goya, I have no idea what Carl's doing today.'

'Okay. So you didn't marry Carl.'

'Actually I did. We'd just finished saying "I do" or whatever when Benjamin got there.'

'Was it a big wedding?'

'Goya, what difference does it make if it was a big wedding?'

'You can't tell me?'

'It was big.'

Goya nodded.

'All the preparations had been made secretly, without Benjamin finding out — Carl's family lived in Santa Barbara and that's where we had it.'

'Bridesmaids?' Goya said.

'What?'

'If it was some rush job,' Goya said, 'I'm thinking you might not have had time to get bridesmaids' dresses and all that.'

'Goya . . .'

'You can't tell me if you had bridesmaids?'

'I had bridesmaids.'

'Okay, go on.'

Elaine looked at her a moment before speaking again. 'So anyway,' she said, 'Benjamin found out about it somehow — I think one of Carl's friends told him . . .'

'Was there a reception?'

'Jesus Christ, Goya.'

'You can't tell me if there was a reception?'

'Goya, how could there be a reception if Benjamin kidnapped me — as you put it — right out of the church?'

'Maybe he let you stop off for it.'

Elaine shook her head. 'What is the point of telling you this?'

'Okay. No reception. What happened next?'

'Monday we went over to the Santa Barbara Court House and I applied for an annulment. In California you can do that if the marriage hasn't been consummated.'

It was quiet for a moment.

'So you and Carl hadn't consummated it.'

uld we have consum

ucking pissed

showed up
u please tell
have consum-

have been rushed.'

uests would have got
h.'
'

picture of
got back
fly had
it was

keep

up at her. 'I don't know
nia law,' she said, 'but I wonder
nsummated it with Carl before
age if that would have had any
n things. Legally.'
n't consummate it with Carl before,
or after the marriage.'
u never did.'
No.'
'Why not?'
'Because I hardly knew him.'
'That never used to stop me.'
'I'm sure it didn't,' Elaine said, 'but my
point is there was no cult.'

Goya nodded. 'So you got it annulled. Then what?'

'Benjamin and I got married and lived

209

.appily ever after. Till now.'

'Where'd you get married?'

'In Reno.'

'And how'd that go?'

'Very smoothly.'

'No hitches.'

'No,' Elaine said. 'They took a
us after the ceremony and when w
to the motel Benjamin noticed hi
been open, but other than that
charming.'

It was quiet for a few moments.

'But Elaine?'

'Yes, Goya.'

'Why was everyone trying so hard to
you and Benjamin apart?'

Again it was quiet.

'If you say there was no cult.'

'I understand your question.'

'It doesn't add up.'

Elaine cleared her throat. 'There was
something else everyone was upset about at
the time.'

'Which was what?'

She looked down at the side of her shoe
resting on Richard Nixon's face. 'Goya,
some things in families are private.'

'We're all in the same family, Elaine.'

'I didn't know that.'

'At least I hope we are.'

'Oh. I guess you mean The Family of Man.'

'Call it what you will.'

Again for a long time it was quiet, till finally Elaine shrugged. 'Why not?' she said. 'It came out that Benjamin and Mother had been consummating their relationship.'

Goya frowned.

'So now you know.'

'You thought they'd been fucking?'

'After Benjamin came home from college, they had an affair.'

'And that's something the cult leader put in your head?'

Elaine got to her feet. 'Thanks for stopping by, Goya.'

'Elaine, how do you think those people get power over you? They make you believe bizarre shit like that to turn you against your family members.'

'Up,' Elaine said, reaching down for her arm.

'They convinced Frieda her grandfather had a contract out on her.'

Elaine began lifting her to her feet.

'Do you mind, for Christ's sake?' Goya pulled her arm away, then stood.

Elaine gestured toward the top of the stairs.

'Elaine, I am just fucking trying to help you.'

'I'm beyond help, Goya.'

'Tell me about it,' she said, starting down the steps. 'But at least out of consideration to the rest of us, get your ass back to a deprogrammer so he can finish the job.'

Garth returned from New York later in the day and his wife told him they would have to prolong their stay because her calming presence was needed for order to be restored in the chaotic household. By then Benjamin had removed the small desk chair from his younger son's room and placed it just underneath the panel in the hallway ceiling. The panel remained in place, though, and no sound came from the other side of it. But this didn't prevent Benjamin from directing his own comments ceilingward, although none of these, including one he made several times during the day — 'What are you pissing in up there, the insulation?' — elicited a response.

Sometimes he provided a running commentary on the events taking place below, which were clearly audible to him when the speakers were in the living room. 'They're talking about you now. They're saying how much they both love you and want you to find the happiness that comes only with inner peace. Now they're doing a chant designed to fill you with everlasting contentment.' He sat listening for a few moments to the chanting, then looked up at the ceiling. 'Is it working?'

The three boys came back into the house at the end of the afternoon and he relayed to Elaine the events of their day.

'Just one spaceman landed. He was cleverly disguised as a policeman and asked the boys why they were standing in the empty pool. Although Matt and Jason were alarmed at his approach, fortunately Aaron easily identified the intruder and addressed him in his native tongue. Nonetheless, the alien demanded to know why they weren't in school and upon receiving Jason's explanation, in English, put in a call to Warren G. Harding, where it was confirmed that they had a valid reason not to be in school. Following this incident the three boys wandered back and forth on the main street of town for several hours, speculating on who was best qualified to govern the various continents.'

But in the absence of any appreciative rejoinders to Benjamin's humorous retelling of these episodes, his enthusiasm for passing them along gradually flagged, and when evening came and a party began taking shape below, he sat listening silently to its progress as Goya went out to their van to bring in some wineskins, and as the children intermittently ran shouting from room to room, and as Garth's guitar was brought out for the group singing of some of the day's popular songs (Benjamin's lips parted slightly at the sound of Nan loudly joining in on a chorus of 'Monday, Monday', one of his and Elaine's favorites, but then his mouth closed again soundlessly).

The odor of marijuana smoke found its way into the upstairs hallway sometime during the evening, but by then the well-known soporific qualities of this substance were of little use to Benjamin, who was slumped in the small chair, dozing on and off despite the raucous goings-on beneath him.

Once during the night Benjamin did have a brief conversation with his wife, which took place after their sons had come up to bed. Jason climbed the stairs first. 'You missed a great one, Dad,' he said, going past his father and to his room.

'Well Jason?' Benjamin said, getting up from his chair as Jason began closing his door.

'Dad, It's after two a.m. I don't think we should let these late-night sessions become a habit.'

Benjamin nodded. 'True. We'll talk about things in the morning.'

Matt came up a few minutes later and stopped outside the door of his room. 'How come you're sitting on my chair?' he said.

'Your mother's in the attic tonight,' Benjamin said. 'I'm sitting down here.'

Matt glanced up at the panel in the ceiling, then back at his father. 'This might be a dumb question.'

'Matt, we're all going to talk in the morning. Right now we need to get whatever sleep we still can.'

Matt looked at him a moment longer. 'I guess Jason told you about the incident,' he said. Then he turned into his room. 'Night.'

He was seated on his bed, reaching down to untie his shoes, when his father arrived in the doorway. 'Oh Dad,' he said, looking up, 'it's you. How's it going?'

'What incident?'

'We can cover it in the morning.'

'Did something happen down there?'

Matt stood again, shoes untied, and walked out past his father and down to the end of the hall. He knocked on his brother's door and, after a few moments, Jason opened it. 'I'm going to bed.'

'Dad wants you to tell him about the

215

incident.'

'You tell him.'

'Boys,' Benjamin said, joining them, 'just tell me what happened so we can all get some sleep.'

'There was a slight situation at the party,' Jason said. 'We handled it as best we could.'

'You're the one who handled it,' Matt said. 'She wasn't talking to me.'

'She was talking to both of us.'

'Who?' Benjamin said.

Matt shook his head. 'I wasn't involved.'

'One for each of us,' Jason said to his brother. 'It was so obvious.'

'Wrong.' Matt shook his head.

'One of what for each of you?' Benjamin said.

'She was just talking to Jason.'

'Look, I don't care who she was talking to,' Benjamin said. 'Did Nan say something to you?'

'Goya,' Matt said.

'Goya.'

'If she was talking to both of us,' Matt said, 'how come you're the only one who answered her?'

'Because you were just standing there with your mouth hanging open.'

'Oh right,' Matt said, nodding. 'Really. My

mouth was really hanging open, wasn't it, Jason?'

'Just tell me what she said,' Benjamin said loudly. 'Forget who she said it to.'

'It was just one word,' Matt said.

'Which was?'

'Thirsty?'

'Thirsty,' Benjamin said.

'With one in each hand,' Jason said, 'which proves she was talking to both of us.'

'How does it?'

'It's self-evident.'

'But she was aiming them both at you.'

'She was aiming one at each of us, you little creep.'

Benjamin nodded. 'I'm getting the picture.'

'Not a pretty one, is it, Dad?' Matt said.

Benjamin held up his hand. 'Okay. Let's be perfectly clear. Goya offered to nurse you.'

'Just him,' Matt said.

'Dad, tell him he's a creep and a liar.'

'She offered to breastfeed you,' Benjamin said. 'Is that right?'

'One of us,' Matt said. 'I won't say which.'

'Just as an aside, Matt,' his father said, 'why are you so fanatical she wasn't talking to you?'

'Because I'm not into that sort of thing.'

'Who said you were?'

'Nobody. I just want to make sure everyone knows I'm not.'

'And everyone does,' his father said. 'Okay?'

'That's all I care about.'

Benjamin turned to his other son. 'What did you say back to her?'

'When she said "Thirsty?'' "

'Right.'

'No thank you.'

'That's true,' Matt said. 'Those were his exact words.'

'No thank you,' Benjamin said.

'That's all that came to mind.'

Their father looked down at the floor a few moments, then back at his older son. 'That was exactly right,' he said. 'The best possible response. Polite and respectful, despite the awkwardness of the situation.'

'It's all I could think of.'

'And was that the end of it?'

'She said one other thing,' Matt said.

'What was that?'

'Don't knock it till you've tried it.'

Benjamin looked back at Jason. 'Did you respond to that?'

'I didn't.'

'Actually you did,' Matt said.

'What did I say?'

'Maybe some other time.'

'Oh right. I did say that.'

'Maybe some other time,' Benjamin said.

'It's just what came to mind.'

Again it was quiet, then Benjamin nodded. 'That was exactly right too,' he said. 'A basically outrageous situation, and yet you had the presence of mind to think of her feelings. Nothing rude. Nothing insensitive. But a response that made clear to her that it was out of the question.' There was a pause. 'So was that the end of it?'

'That was the incident in its entirety,' Matt said.

Again for a long time it was quiet. 'Time for bed,' Benjamin said at last. 'When things settle down again it will be fascinating to go into all the cultural questions this incident brings up. But right now you need your sleep. You both handled a highly challenging social situation with great skill.'

'I didn't handle it.'

'Well your brother handled it with great skill. I commend you, Jason.'

'Thanks, Dad.' He went into his room.

Matt was frowning 'Dad?'

'Yes, Matt.'

'How does saying "Maybe some other time" make it clear it's out of the question?'

It was a minute or two after Benjamin had

resumed his post on the little chair that there was a click over his head. He got to his feet and looked up as the panel was lowered several inches. 'Elaine,' he said, 'it's about time.'

'What was that about?' she said.

'What?'

'What were you talking about?'

'The party's over. Come down now.' Benjamin reached up for the rope but the panel went back up into the ceiling. He lowered his arm. 'Elaine?'

A few moments later the crack appeared again.

'I am not up here because of the party. I am up here until I have my house back.'

Benjamin nodded.

'What were the three of you arguing about?'

'No one was arguing. We were just discussing the party.'

'You were arguing.'

'Elaine, if you couldn't hear what we were saying, how could you tell we were arguing?'

'I could tell it was a heated discussion. I couldn't make out the words.'

'I was commending Jason on his behavior at the party.'

'What behavior?'

'There was a minor incident and I was

commending him on the mature way he handled it.'

'What was the incident?'

Benjamin looked down at the chair.

'Benjamin.'

'I'm trying to remember.'

'You can't remember an incident on which you commended him for his maturity three minutes ago?'

'Some exchange with Goya,' he said, looking up again. 'I think that was it.'

'What exchange with Goya?'

'Elaine, if you will come down here we can discuss it properly.'

'What exchange with her?'

'Just some silly thing.'

'What silly thing?'

'Some silly thing she said to them.'

'Which was?'

Again Benjamin frowned down toward the chair, then looked up again. 'It's too insignificant to bring to mind.'

'All right,' she said, as the crack above Benjamin's head began to close. 'Well, why don't you tell me when you can remember?'

'She made them an offer.'

'Offer?'

'Elaine, it was so trivial. Possibly it could be blown out of proportion. The point is how well Jason handled it.'

'An offer of what?'

'Milk.'

'What?'

'Elaine.'

'I didn't hear what you said — you were mumbling. Say it again.'

'A glass of milk.'

Again it was quiet. 'She offered them a glass of milk?'

'Oh wait a minute,' he said, holding up his hand. 'No. I had part of that wrong.'

'What?'

'Elaine, the thing to concentrate on here is the incredible poise Jason exhibited in dealing with an extremely difficult social situation.'

'Let me guess,' she said. 'You had the glass part wrong.'

'That's the part I had wrong. But the point is how proud you would have been of —'

The panel above Benjamin slammed shut and there was a sharp metallic click.

When Elaine came down next morning Benjamin was still dozing in the chair and the narrow wooden stairway hit the top of his head, waking him. He got up, pulling the chair out of the way so she could lower the stairs the rest of the way. When she had reached the bottom she pushed the stairs back up into the ceiling and then turned to smile at him. 'Good morning.'

He looked back at her, then nodded.

'How did you sleep?' she said.

'I've had better.'

'Me too.' She went into the bedroom.

Several moments later he followed.

'Matt and Jason have been talking about seeing *The Towering Inferno*,' she said over the sound of running water. 'Do you know if that's still playing on Central Avenue?'

'I don't.'

'I thought it might be fun for me to take the two of them and Aaron over to see it. I think that theatre starts its showings at noon or so, doesn't it?' She came out several minutes later, drying her face off with a towel. 'Don't you think that would be fun for them?'

'It would be.'

'I'm sure it's still there,' she said. 'I think it just opened last week.' She put the towel on the bed. 'Then after the movie I'll come back and drop Aaron off.' She smiled at him as she approached him, still standing in the doorway. 'Excuse me.'

He stepped aside so she could go into the hall.

'What do you mean?' he said as she went

223

to the end of the hall.

She stopped and turned back to him. 'About what?'

'You'll drop Aaron off.'

'So he can rejoin his family.'

Benjamin nodded. 'Well that's good.'

'So is everything clear?' she said, still smiling at him.

'Perfectly. But it was just an odd way to put it.'

'What was odd about it?'

'I mean, you said "Drop Aaron off",' Benjamin said, making a gesture.

'That's what I'll do.'

'Well yes. But it was just a slightly strange way to put it.'

'Why?'

'Because it made it sound like . . . you know . . . you're going to drop Aaron off . . .'

She continued smiling.

'But you know,' he said, 'like you won't be coming in yourselves.'

She nodded.

'You won't.'

'Not if Mother's still here.'

'Oh, okay. I see what you were getting at.'

'So is it all clear to you now?'

'Well not exactly.'

'What's not clear yet?'

'Okay, if Mother's still here when you get

back from the movie, you'll drop Aaron off and do what? The rest of you.'

'Go on along.'

'Go on along?'

'That's right.'

He shook his head. 'This is disjointed.'

'I thought it was clear.'

'It is. But now it's disjointed.'

'What's disjointed about it?'

'You'll come back after the movie and drop Aaron off, but if Mother's still here the rest of you will go on along.'

'You have it.'

'Go along where?'

'We'll let you know when we're settled.' She walked the rest of the way down the stairs.

There was a brief squeaking noise as toilet paper was pulled from its roll. Then it was quiet for a moment before the loud sound of flushing. Nan stepped out of her room. 'Oh Ben,' she said, looking up at him, 'I didn't know you were there.'

'May we talk?'

'I was just coming up. Did the others get off?'

'We need to talk.'

'Wasn't that a good idea of Elaine's?' She turned sideways to go past him in the doorway. 'Taking the boys to the movie. Of course she's the one who needs the break. Ben, I am getting so worried about that girl. She just doesn't know her own limits, does she?' She went into the living room.

'Nan.'

'Do you know when the movie lets out?'

'Three fifty-seven.'

In one corner of the room a sleeping bag was in a heap, partially covering an air mattress. 'You know, I have grown so fond of that little family,' she said, walking to it. 'Honestly, I never thought I could. But Ben, I mean really.' She picked up the sleeping bag, held it out to shake, then folded it in half. 'There is a bare minimum, isn't there.' She pushed the plastic mattress all the way into the corner with her foot and then rested the bag on it.

'The three of them won't be coming back into the house,' he said.

She straightened up to look up at him.

'If you're still here.'

It was quiet a moment, then she shook her head.

'If you're still here when they come back from the movie, Elaine will drop Aaron off and then they'll go on.'

She looked at him a moment longer, then bent down to pick a pair of Levis up from the floor. 'Go on where?'

'She'll tell me when they're settled.'

Nan folded the Levis to place on the sleeping bag.

'And so the best thing right now,' Benjamin said, 'for the sake of your grandchildren, whose lives will be thrown into utter turmoil if this happens, is for me to help you get organized so you've left by the time they return.'

'By three fifty-seven,' she said.

'Yes.'

'Well then of course it takes — how long will it take them to drive back from Central Avenue?'

'That's not the point.'

'Well no, but I'm just trying to calculate how much time I have.' She picked up a backpack from beside the wall to put on the mattress.

'Nan, don't keep worrying about their things.'

'Ben, somebody has to.'

'They will.'

'But they won't, Ben, that's my whole point. I mean, they're as free as the breeze and how refreshing that is, but as I was telling Goya just this morning, you can be a free spirit and all that, but even free spirits have to wash out their underpants once in a while.' She picked up a large bra from the floor but Benjamin walked across the room and took it away from her. 'I'm making a little pile,' she said. 'Just drop it on that.'

'There isn't time for this.'

'For what?'

'This.'

'Ben, how long does it take to drop a brassiere?' She took it back from him, folded it in half and set it on the other things. 'Oh, by the way, you do know about the new plan, don't you?' She pointed at a pajama top on the floor behind him. 'Hand me that.'

'What new plan?'

'Just hand me that, can you?'

Benjamin reached over with his foot and pushed the item of clothing over to the others. 'What plan?'

'The Lewises'.'

'Which is what?'

'They're leaving after all,' she said as she bent down for the pajamas. 'I mean, I sort of gave them a nudge, to be honest. Don't worry, I was tactful, but here we all are standing by and watching poor Elaine go under for the third time trying to manage this great horde of people, so when Goya mentioned that Garth's started worrying about a heart attack — can you imagine, someone of his age — I took the opportunity of saying maybe the time had come for them to heed the call of the wild.'

Benjamin nodded. 'Okay. Well that's good.'

'Goya and Neffi will spend a couple hours down by the river. He's coming back from the city a little earlier today, but not for a while, so by the time our little family gets back they'll be all packed up and waiting in the van for Aaron.' She looked over at a shirt draped across the back of the sofa.

'It's not your little family, Nan.'

'What isn't?'

'Us.'

'Well whose ever little family it is,' she said, walking to the shirt, 'Elaine will be able to take a great deep breath when she doesn't —'

He walked quickly to her, took the shirt out of her hand to bunch up and then threw it over onto the pile. 'What's the situation with your flight?'

'My flight?'

'Do you not understand, Nan, what is happening here?!'

'Well yes,' she said. 'Elaine's swamped with —'

'Elaine could cope quite comfortably with ten Lewis families.'

'Ten.' She laughed. 'Now you're giving me a heart attack.' Nan reached over the back of the sofa toward a sandal on one of the cushions, but Benjamin took hold of her wrist to stop her from picking it up. They stood looking down at his fingers around her wrist for a moment, then he released them and took the sandal to throw over onto the pile.

'Your flight situation,' he said.

'I have a tentative.'

'Tentative what?'

'Things got so crazy yesterday,' she said. 'The poor airline people didn't know if they were coming or going, so Elaine left it that if I didn't get to the airport by check-in time yesterday — which I didn't, obviously — they would hold space on the same flight today, up to a certain point.'

'What point?'

Nan stepped to the large window overlooking the street.

'Nan.'

'Yes, Ben.'

'To what point will they hold space today?'

Looking out the window, Nan didn't answer right away. 'Ben, you have to come and see this. Your neighbor across the street has one of these newfangled garage-opening things and it doesn't seem to be working. He keeps aiming at his garage door and —'

'What point!'

'What point what?' she said, turning around, smiling.

'Will they hold space on the flight?!'

'Nine this evening,' she said, 'so I have all the time in the world.'

'Not until the movie's over do you have all the time in the world!'

She looked back down at the pile of clothing. 'Ben, you know what I think Elaine must have meant. She's so confused at the moment, I'm sure she meant she couldn't face coming back inside if the Lewises were still here.'

He stared at her.

'A slip of the tongue, that's what it was. Well, who can blame her?'

'I'm begging you, Nan,' he said.

'Begging me?'

'Yes.'

'What a strange thing to say, Ben.'

'Oh dear God, please leave before she gets back.'

For a long time the two of them looked at each other, then Nan's gaze fell to a small table against the wall beside Benjamin. 'Last night at the party,' she said, 'Matt and Jason were telling me about the project you all did learning to play poker.' She walked to the table and picked up a pack of cards. 'They were so cute.' She carried the cards to the sofa, seating herself on the end cushion and then holding the cards down on the center cushion to shuffle. 'Here they were, teaching me how to play five-card draw.' She shuffled them again. 'Ben, when Elaine was growing up, her father and I took turns with our friends going around to each other's homes for poker evenings. I don't think there was once I didn't clean the rest of them out. They finally had to give me a handicap.' She shuffled a third time. 'And here was little Matt explaining to me the difference between a full house and a royal flush.' She smiled. 'That was so sweet. Of course I didn't let on.' She looked up at him. 'Let's have a hand or two.'

'Jesus Christ, Nan.'

'Don't worry, not for money.'

'Nan, as degrading as this is for me, I am literally begging you to let my marriage survive.'

She tilted her head slightly as she looked back at him. 'You're saying the strangest things, Ben.' She patted the far cushion. 'Sit down. We'll just have one quick hand and then I'll throw my things together. Oh, and bring me my purse.' She pointed at it, on the little table where the cards had been. 'Don't worry, we aren't playing for money. This is something else.'

'One quick hand.'

'My purse, Ben.'

'One quick hand and then you leave.'

She glanced at her watch. 'Ben, hurry up, I want to get started for the airport.'

He watched as she began dealing cards onto the center cushion, then picked up the purse and carried it across to her.

'Just put it on the floor.'

He set it down beside the sofa, then seated himself at the other end from her.

'Jason was telling me the point of your poker project was to study how people bluff each other — Ben, I just love how you take the everyday things of life and turn them into an educational experience for the boys.' She finished dealing and held up her cards. 'But I just want to say I don't think you learned your own lesson very well if you can't tell that Elaine has no intention of walking out on you.'

'She doesn't bluff.'

'Pick up your hand, Ben.'

He picked it up. 'I'll stay.'

'Well at least see what you have.' She studied her own cards, then removed two to place on the cushion before drawing two from the pile to replace them with. 'What do you have?' she said.

He set them face-up on the cushion.

'Darling, you didn't even look at them.'

'I stayed.'

'How can you stay if you don't even know what you have?'

'It's time to get started.'

She shook her head. 'Ben, that wasn't a game. Really. That's insulting.'

'We played.'

She gathered the cards together. 'You deal this time,' she said, holding them out.

'Go, Nan.'

'Ben, I want to end my visit on a high note,' she said. 'Not some phony game so I'll just be thinking all you wanted was to get me out the door.'

'That's all we want.'

She continued holding them in front of him. 'Benjamin, it's not even one-thirty yet. You said they get out at four.'

'You said one game.'

'A proper game, yes.'

He looked down at the cards.

'Anyway, there's something I need to show you.'

It was quiet a few moments.

'Ben, deal. We're wasting time.'

He took them from her, placed them on the cushion and quickly shuffled them once. As he dealt them Nan reached down into her purse beside the sofa and removed a small blue envelope. She rested it on her knee.

'Nan, don't start up on anything.'

'Start up on what?'

'Whatever it is,' he said, nodding at the envelope. 'Put it away. One proper game and then you're gone. I'm sorry to be crude.'

'Ben, you couldn't be crude if you tried.' She watched as he began dealing the cards. 'But all right then. We'll just take one thing at a time.'

'The card game is the only thing we're taking, Nan.' He finished dealing five cards to each of them, then picked up his hand.

'Men can only do one thing at a time,' she said as she picked hers up. 'Did you know that?'

He shook his head.

'I read that somewhere. A study. Women can do all kinds of things at once but men can only do one.'

Benjamin quickly went through his cards, removing three to put on the cushion before replacing them with three from the pile.

'Hmm,' Nan said, studying her cards. 'Hmm. Hmm. Hmm.'

'Two pairs,' Benjamin said, setting his face-up between them.

She frowned.

'What do you have?'

'Ben, I haven't even decided what to put back yet.'

'Well could you?'

'You're showing me your hand even before I decide what to put back. Good Lord, I hope you weren't the one who taught the boys how to play.'

'Nan.'

'Ben, I'm sorry, but we are going to play a proper hand.' She returned her cards to the pile. 'I'll deal this one.'

'We're finished.'

'You showed your cards early.'

'It was sloppy playing on my part, but it was a proper game. The astute poker player takes advantage of the mistakes of an opponent, which I assume you will do. You won.'

'But I hope the astute poker player doesn't take advantage of an opponent exhibiting brain death.'

'You won, Nan,' he said, getting up from the sofa. 'Game's over.'

They looked at each other a few moments, then Nan picked up the envelope from her knee.

'Put it away.'

'You don't know what it is yet.'

'And I don't need to.'

'Ben, I brought it all the way from California to show you.'

'Take it all the way back.'

After a moment she opened the flap of the envelope and took out a folded sheet of stationery.

'Put . . . it . . . a . . . way.'

'Ben, you're being so rude.'

'I thought I couldn't be rude if I tried.'

'That was crude. Listen. To make up for your little lapse in manners, why don't you just let me very quickly go into this so I can be on my way.'

'Quickly quickly quickly then.'

Again she looked at her watch. 'Ben, the movie hasn't even started over there yet. Well, maybe the trailers.' She unfolded the letter. 'This was sent to me last year by a stockbroker friend. Sadly, we've parted company since then, but we were hot and heavy at the time.'

'Quickly quickly.'

'Don't you want to sit down again?'

'Quickly.'

'Ben, I'm going as quickly as I can. Where was I?'

'Stockbroker friend. Hot and heavy.'

'That's right.'

He made a large circular motion with his hand.

'Jesus Christ, Benjamin, the goddamn movie is just now starting.'

'They may come back early.'

'Why would they do that?'

'The theatre may be full.'

'In the middle of the day on a Wednesday?'

'One of them may get sick.'

'You'll make your deadline, Ben.' She set the piece of stationery on her knee and reached back into her purse. 'I have a couple other related things to show you,' she said, bringing up two more pieces of paper. 'I won't need to leave these with you, but they'll give you some background if you're not familiar with the scandal. Let's see now. How shall we do this?'

'Just do it.'

'Ben,' she said, looking up, 'if she's given you the ultimatum that she'll leave you if I'm still here after the movie lets out at four, and if for any unforeseen reason she has to come back early, and I'm still here, she will make the adjustment and allow you the additional time to throw me out.'

He looked back without answering.

'Won't she? She's a sensible girl — one of the many admirable traits she got from her mother — and she's not going to be so rash as to throw her marriage away because of the change in a movie timetable, now is she?'

He nodded at the letter.

'You do her a disservice, Ben,' she said. 'Now. Let me see. First of all, were you aware of the big Westinghouse scandal out there last year?'

'I may have seen something about it.'

She held up a newspaper clipping. 'In case you hadn't.'

'I had.'

'God, it was huge out there. Someone was running for some office and this hit at the same time and the public was all up in arms about white-collar crime blah blah blah and this politician made a great stink about it and people were going to jail left, right and center . . .'

'Nan.'

'Yes, Ben.'

'Get to the point, whatever the hell it is.'

'You know about insider trading,' she said.

'Know about it?'

'What it is.'

'Yes.'

'So we won't worry about this then,' she said, putting down the clipping. 'From the *Los Angeles Times*. Reviewing the whole history of the matter, but also giving a good definition, I thought, of what insider trading is, in case you didn't know. But as you say, you do.'

239

'Th
She
make
'Wel
'To 
'Get
She 
is my
wasn't
though
now I'n
to keep
'Nan,
shit?'
'Well l
'Just g
the hell t
'The le
knee. Aft
held it be
idiot wou
writing w
mystery t
reputable
was conce
'Love turr
That's the
'Nan.'
'You wan
'With gre

to sell all my shares — I had a mountain[
them. Which I did. And walked away w[
over a hundred thousand dollars.'

'Congratulations.'

'Then a week or so later, all that horses[
started hitting the fan out there. Well B[
we were sweating bullets, as you can im[
ine. But somehow he kept me out of[
Finagled his books in some way, God kn[
how. I mean the man really is brilliant, B[
I will say that for him, even though his m[
is mush.' She shrugged. 'But he did so[
thing with numbers and somehow the wh[
storm passed right over my head.'

Benjamin nodded. 'Is that it then?'

'Ben, if you keep interrupting we'll ne[
get through it.'

Benjamin reached up and pinched his[
together.

'Where was I now? Oh yes. So after[
broke up, the man went into a complete[
utter tailspin over this.' She waved the[
ter. 'I mean, I thought he was going to h[
a nervous breakdown over it. I'm not m[
ing that up. "Find it!" In the middle of[
night. Seriously. In the middle of the g[
damn night. I told him I'd lost it. "Fin[
Jesus Christ, you have to find it! Don't s[
looking for it until you find it!" Well I fir[
told him I'd found it and burned it. "Bur[

242

it! Oh God! I told you to give it back to me! Not destroy it!" What it was, Ben, he thought I might just pretend to destroy it. Which of course is what I did.' She looked back at the letter. 'I wasn't his little skunk any more at that point.'

'Finished?' Benjamin said.

'Well yes, in a way,' she said, 'but we haven't decided whether I'm going to leave it with you or not.'

'We have.'

'Judging by the other prison terms they were handing out, he'd probably get fifteen years and I'd get ten or so. I mean, Ben, it was an absolute frenzy out there. I kid you not. And I'm quite sure they'd feel they had to be consistent if anything about this popped up again, even though it's all blown over by now in the press.'

Benjamin watched her pick up the other papers. 'If you don't need any help downstairs,' he said, 'I'll call the cab.'

'But really,' she said, 'can you believe ten years?' Not looking away from him she reached down to push the papers back into her purse beside the sofa. 'For selling a few shitty little shares when you feel like it?' She got to her feet. 'Sometimes I have to ask myself — what is this world coming to?' She reached down to her hip to unfasten the

243

clasp of the skirt she was wearing. 'By the way,' she said, letting the skirt drop around her legs to the floor, 'this isn't what it looks like.' She stepped out of the skirt. 'But I mean for ten years you'd think they'd at least let you do something interesting,' she said, bending down to close her purse and pick up the skirt. 'Like poison somebody.' She carried the purse and skirt across the room to put on the small table. 'This isn't what it looks like,' she said again, unbuttoning her blouse.

Benjamin stood looking at her from across the room.

'You look a little pale, Ben.' After removing the blouse and resting it on the other things, she reached behind herself to unfasten the clasp of her bra.

'Don't do this.'

She bent forward slightly to let the straps of the bra fall down over her arms. 'Well it's your climate of course. Everyone back here looks pale.' She set the bra on the table and pushed her panties down over her legs and stepped out of them. 'The four of you really need to come out for a visit the first chance you get and soak up some of our good California sunshine.'

'I will run out of this house,' Benjamin said.

'You'll what?'

'Run out of this house.'

She put the panties on the table.

'Put them back on.'

'Ben, how many times do I have to tell you this isn't what it looks like.'

'It's what it looks like,' he said.

'Well it's not. But I can see how you'd get that impression.'

'I'm running out of this house now,' he said, starting toward the door.

'Ben, will you please let me explain what's happening here?'

'I know what's happening here.'

'Well obviously you don't.'

'I can't believe this.'

'Well I can't either. A fully grown man threatening to run out of his house.'

'I cannot fucking believe this is happening.'

'Elaine must have been the one I mentioned this to,' she said, shaking her head and then running her fingers through her hair. 'You must not have been there.'

'I'm running.'

'Ben, I've stopped wearing anything when I'm at home now, that's all this is. One day it just hit me — why in hell am I going around wrapped up in cloth and elastic all day, uncomfortable as a mummy? It's my

245

own home, for Christ sake, I'll do what I want in it.'

He watched her bend down to remove one of her shoes.

'So I turned up the thermostat and off they came.' She removed the other shoe. 'And I haven't had a stitch on since that day. At home, that is. I'm still a bit reticent at the supermarket.' She placed the two shoes side by side on the floor. 'Want to hear a funny story? You'll love this, Ben. When I started taking it off around the house, a year or so ago, this little Costa Rican cleaning lady was coming in once a week, and the first day she came in when I was *au naturel* we'd be going back and forth around the house and every time we'd pass she'd give me this dark, disapproving look.' Nan turned her arm so that she could look down at one of her elbows, then brushed it off. 'I felt like saying, "Well fuck you, please, I live here." But of course I don't speak Spanish — well, "Clean this again," that's about it.' She looked back at Benjamin. 'So then the next week she comes in again, still lurking around all day with her little dust rag and scowling looks, but after she's gone I go in my bedroom and there's this Bible resting on the table.' Nan laughed. 'Is that a classic?' When she finished laughing she lowered her gaze back to Benjamin. 'So you see there's no need for anyone to run out of their house.'

He looked back at her without speaking.

'Is there?'

Still he didn't answer.

'Is there?' she said again.

'Nan,' he said.

'Yes, Ben.'

'I'm not going to run out of my house.'

'Well I hope not.'

'There's no need to.'

'I never thought there was.'

'What there's a need for,' he said, 'is for you to get something out of your head I can't believe is in it.'

Nan put her hands under her breasts and lifted them slightly. 'Not to embarrass you, Ben, but how do you think I've held up over the years?'

'Did you hear what I said?'

She looked down at one of the breasts in her hand. 'I get the feeling you don't want to tell me how you think I've held up.'

'That feeling is accurate.'

'Well if you change your mind,' she said, 'all I ask is that somewhere in your answer you include the words "not" and "sagging".'

'From the very beginning this is something you've been planning,' he said.

'What is, darling?'

'From the minute you got here. From before you got here. Nan, may I just think for a moment?'

'Think?'

'For a moment.'

She shrugged. 'Of course. I'm thinking's biggest fan.'

Benjamin pushed his hands down into his pockets and looked at the floor.

'I guess thinking and talking at the same time isn't an option.'

He kept his eyes on the floor.

'Yes, well that's what the study said.'

'You're making this a fucking condition,' he said finally, looking up.

'Making what a condition?'

'You actually think you can make sex a condition for your leaving.'

She looked back at him a moment. 'Did somebody say sex?'

Benjamin began shaking his head. 'You are beyond depraved, Mrs Robinson.'

She smiled.

'Nan.'

It was quiet for a few moments.

'Okay,' he said, removing his hands from his pockets, 'let me think.'

'You already did that.'

'So what's that all about?' he said, pointing at the purse on the table.

'My purse?'

'Some goddamn letter from a stockbroker.'

'That's for you to have afterwards.'

'There's not going to be any fucking "afterwards", Nan. But what kind of twisted thing is that all about?'

'The letter?'

'The letter.'

'I don't know,' she said. 'For one thing, it could send me to jail.'

He lowered his arm. 'And you're going to leave it with me.'

'Afterwards.'

'Why?'

She shrugged. 'A keepsake.'

'Keepsake.'

'Ben, do you want to hear another funny cleaning-lady story?'

'One funny cleaning-lady story a day is my quota.' He looked back at the table.

'Different cleaning lady. This one's even funnier.'

'Okay, you're going to leave a self-incriminatory letter with me.'

'Ben, this will lighten the mood.'

'Why would you want to do that?'

'What happened was that she locked herself inside my car. It's one of those new itomatic self-locking things and you can pen it from the inside but you have to know how. Which she didn't.'

'No more cleaning-lady howlers, Nan.'

'Ben, try to picture this.'

'I need to picture what the letter's about.'

'Okay, I sent her out to empty my ashtray and she locked herself inside. It was a rainy day and the car windows were all steamed up.'

He frowned, continuing to look at her purse.

'And when I went out to see what was taking so long she'd written "Help" on the inside of one of the windows.'

'Wait a minute,' Benjamin said.

'But she was dumb as a box of rocks,' Nan said, 'so she'd written it the right way around for her, but from the outside you couldn't read it.'

'So you won't tell Elaine,' he said, looking back at her.

'Tell Elaine what?'

'I'm right, aren't I?'

'About what?'

'If I have the letter to hold over your head I can be sure you'll never tell Elaine,' he said. 'That's it, isn't it?'

'More or less.'

'You'll put me in a position to blackmail you.'

'Well who gave me that idea?' she said.

'What?'

'Why was I summoned back here?'

Benjamin shook his head. 'Now where are we going?'

'I figured . . . you know . . . a school principal for openers. Maybe he'd like to throw a mother-in-law into the mix.'

'That's slightly different.'

She shrugged. 'If you say so.'

Benjamin held up his hand. 'Let's stay on the subject. Okay. Now in what passes for your mind the only conceivable reason I wouldn't have sex with you is that Elaine might find out about it. And if I don't have to worry about that, off come the pants.'

'Or just drop them down,' she said. 'I don't want to make too big a thing of it.'

'But there isn't any other reason I wouldn't do it.'

'Than Elaine finding out? I doubt it.'

'My feelings for her would of course not stop me.'

'They might slow you down.'

'But I'd want you out of here so badly I'd override them.'

She nodded.

'Our lives have been turned into such shit

251

that when presented with this simple way of everything going back to normal, in your mind there's no way I'll be able to turn it down.'

'I'd kill for a cigarette right now,' she said. 'I suppose your and Elaine's policy about smoking in the house are the same. Well, we can discuss that when she's gone.'

'So what we have here is that the only way I'm going to get my wife back is to be unfaithful to her.'

'We have that.'

'That's not what we have here,' he said.

'I think you'll find it is.'

'No, because you can plant yourself here and my family can break up and the years can pass and the world can finally come to an end and it still won't happen.'

'That you fuck me.'

'That I fuck you.'

'I guess we'll have to see.'

'You'll have to see,' Benjamin said. 'I already know.'

They stood looking at each other a few moments, then Benjamin held out his hand.

'What,' she said.

'Did you want to shake hands?'

'Not particularly. I had a little more than that in mind.'

'We're saying goodbye now, Nan.'

252

'Who is?'

'You and I.'

'I'm not going anywhere,' she said.

'I'm aware of that.'

'You're leaving?'

'No, I'm not going anywhere either.'

'Then what's this,' she said, nodding at his hand.

'We're saying goodbye now,' he said again.

'But no one's going anywhere.'

'No one is, no.'

'Ben, this sounds a little ominous.'

'Goodbye, Nan.' He lowered his hand.

'Jesus, you make it sound like you're about to go in and get out the carving knife.'

Benjamin stepped to the large bay window at the front of the room. Across the street, Ted Rigney and several of Benjamin's other neighbors were gathered in front of the Rigneys' garage. One of them was holding a small device in his hand and pointing it at the garage as they all watched the garage door go slowly up. When the garage was all the way open, he handed the device to the next neighbor, who pointed it at the garage, and then they all watched as the door slowly came back down again. The next neighbor took the device.

Benjamin turned away from the window.

'So where do we go from here?' Nan said.

253

When the Braddocks had moved into Elaine's father's house they had cleared out all his furniture and replaced it with things that were more to their own taste, but there was one piece, a high-backed chair, which Elaine had wanted to keep as a way of having something of her father's always before them to remember him by.

Benjamin walked over to the chair, which was in the far corner of the room, and seated himself.

'You and Elaine have done such cute things with this room,' she said. 'I want to leave it just the way it is. But that thing goes out on the curb for the first collection.'

He looked back at her but didn't answer.

'The chair,' she said.

He continued to look at her but didn't respond.

'I had to look at that eyesore for twenty-three years, Ben, and I don't think I sat in it once. In fact I know I didn't.'

On the floor in front of the chair was a small round throw rug. Nan looked down at it. 'Good idea, Ben. Let's both take a load off.' She lowered herself down onto the rug, then stretched out her legs, putting her arms behind her and leaning back on them. 'So how will it work then, Ben?' she said. 'I mean, will I stay down below? Or will you

254

let me move up to one of the boy's rooms? I really do love my cozy little nook, but even after it was painted baby blue I still have to say I find cinder blocks a tad forbidding.' She looked at one of her feet, moving it slowly in a circle. 'And of course no window. I'm sure you don't want your star boarder coming down with a case of claustrophobia.'

Benjamin made no response.

'You don't want that, do you Ben?' she said, looking up at him.

There was the sound of a car passing in the street.

'Ben?'

When again he failed to answer, even though looking evenly back at her as she spoke, she turned her eyes upward and said, 'Oh dear, I think I'm getting the silent treatment.'

But he made no response to that comment either.

The chair Elaine had kept from her father's belongings was one, she knew, that also had come down to him from his own parents, and so not only did she feel it was important in that it would keep her father in their minds, she felt it was significant also — incongruous as it appeared among the present-day furnishings that surrounded it — that the generation of her grandparents also was represented to them in this way as they went about their daily lives.

It was several minutes before Nan spoke again.

'Do you keep in touch with your parents, Ben?'

He looked down at the thick wooden arm of the chair and at a pattern of leaves and flowers that was carved into the dark polished wood.

'I know your mother had that terrible breakdown after our little — what should I call it? — fling I guess is the best word, and I heard they moved up to Idaho. But they just fell off the map as far as I was concerned.' Her foot became still. 'We were always so close, weren't we, the two families. Ben, do you remember that summer — you probably won't, you must have been Matt's age — but our two families rented a beach house together.' She frowned. 'Where was that — Laguna, that was it. And the families would take turns going down during the summer months to use it. But one weekend — I think it was someone's birthday, your father's it must have been, but we were all down there together, one hot Saturday afternoon — we'd all carried our baskets and umbrellas and everything down to the sand. And I remember how you and Elaine

256

kept running down to the ocean, and you were trying to make this crown for her.' She laughed. 'Out of sand. This dripping wet sand. And you'd both come walking back up to where we were all sitting on our towels to show us, little Elaine walking very straight to try and keep it from falling off. But every time the two of you got back the sand had slid down over her hair and onto her shoulders — it was so sweet, the two of you coming back to show us time and again, and each time the wet sand from the crown all down over her eyes and face, the two of you had us all in stitches. I have a picture of that somewhere, Ben, I'll have to see if I can dig it out. But I'm sure you wouldn't remember. Actually, I think you might have been younger than Matt then. Do you have any recollection of that summer?'

Benjamin was studying the back of his hand as it rested on the arm of the chair.

'And then it all seemed such a shame somehow, didn't it?' Nan said, again looking up at the ceiling. 'What happened later. Such a waste.' She smiled as she looked back down at him. 'Well, you be sure and give them my love next time you talk, won't you?'

But Benjamin said nothing.

For an hour Benjamin remained in the

chair with Nan several yards away from him on the round rug on the floor. At first she sat with her arms behind herself, leaning back against her hands, but then she lay down on her back, opening her legs towards him in a V, sometimes bending them at the knees to slowly open and close as she lay looking up at the ceiling. Finally she turned on her side, propping herself up on an elbow and running her finger around in little circles and other designs on the wooden floor beside her.

When the hour had nearly passed she looked up and said, 'Tell you what, Ben. Maybe we've accomplished all we can on this visit. We've broken the ice again after all these years. Such a good time I've had, getting reacqainted with my little angels. Elaine needs some time now to get her feet back on the ground, and I'm afraid my poor geraniums must be missing me terribly. So why don't I call a cab now, and we'll all pat ourselves on the back for making the brand-new start you wanted us to make when I first got here?'

But he made no response.

'How does that sound, Ben?'

Again he said nothing.

'Ben?'

He kept his eyes on the floor.

Then at last she got to her feet.

'God,' she said, walking across the room toward the kitchen, 'I'd forgotten what a smug little self-righteous arrogant bastard you always were.' She went through the doorway, looking up at a list of numbers that were Scotch-taped onto the wall beside the phone, then dialled one of them. 'I need a taxi for JFK,' she said. There was a pause. 'In Hastings. Let me get the number here for you.' She stepped back so she could look out at Benjamin again. 'Ben, what number are you here on Willard?'

He looked at her without speaking.

'Your house number. I'm on the phone with the taxi.'

He continued silently to look back at her.

'Ben, give me the damn address.'

When he still didn't answer she put her hand over the mouthpiece of the receiver and took a step into the living room. 'If you want me the fuck out of here so badly, give me your goddamn address so I can tell the taxi where to come.'

It was almost a full minute that Benjamin sat looking quietly back at her as she glared at him from the doorway.

Then finally she stepped back into the kitchen, removing her hand from the mouthpiece and returning the receiver to

259